THE ACCUSED

FLABIA THEMBEKA

TRILOGY PUBLISHING
Tustin, CA

First originally published by Trilogy Publishing 2018
Cover Design by La'Marr Collins

ISBN 978-1-64088-061-0 (Paperback)
ISBN 978-1-64088-062-7 (Digital)

Printed in the United States of America

FOREWORD

I AM EXCITED ABOUT the release of this new book. I must say that Flabia Thembeka has the most unique gift I have ever seen.

I have a knowing in my heart that it is no accident you are about to read this book, regardless of how the copy came to you. Flabia explores what makes people 'tick,' squints at the blurring of lines between good and bad, crime and human nature. The Accused is a powerful and complex story with an intensity drawn out through each page. An excellent story about betrayal, forgiveness, and the powerful unconditional love of God.

A beautifully written, perfectly populated, edge-of-your-seat story, "The Accused" is not to be missed!"

Pastor Walter Gillespie,
Chosen Tabernacle Ministries

If Flabia, or June, as she is known by those around her, were a ride at an amusement park, she would undoubtedly be a roller coaster. The evidence of this is very clear by the footprints of herself left on this book: "THE ACCUSED". It takes you to the highest highs and the lowest lows reflecting her knowledge to tell a captivating story and hold your attention. Her intensity levels are evident in her attention to detail, helping to carousel your imagination off to a distant place while painting a very vivid picture. Most importantly, she draws you in with the story like a roller coaster on the incline waiting for the drop that takes your breath away with her twists in the plot. Each one feeds off the other like the buildup of the speed on a coaster as you float out of your seat on its decline. Then every turn keeps you from being able to be situated in your seat. After you finish the book, it's like the end of the ride: you walk away with your mind blown as if you just went on the adventure of a lifetime. While you are walking away, the drawing sensation to do it again penetrates every fiber of your being. Yes, "THE ACCUSED" is a very good book, but it also gives a glimpse of the person; her character and talents and the driving force enveloping her to fulfill her destiny. Read this book "THE ACCUSED" and get a glimpse of her; the writer. I promise you, that you will never regret it.

Lawrence Spivey

CHAPTER

1

JUST NORTH OF THE great windy city known as Chicago, Illinois, lies a quaint suburban town named Evanston. Friendly and enriched in culture, Evanston is home to the great Northwestern University. People from all over come to attend this college. There is a lot to be said about small towns and the secrets that they may hide. If you were to take a tour of Evanston and happen upon the prestigious Colfax Street, you would see there are definitely no shortages of the *crème de la crème* estates. As a matter of fact, in the midst of them sits the famous three-storied Osbourne mansion. It was built in 1901, with impeccable design and breath-taking antiques. It now unravels with an unexpected turn of events.

It is 5 a.m. on a cold and windy Thursday morning, yet Teddy is already up, dressed, and in his office. He is never out of bed at this time of day, unless it is an emergency. Teddy has been nervously pacing the floors and talking to himself. Literally, Teddy has carried on a full conversation, like a mad man, for at least forty-five minutes, in anticipation of his visitor's arrival.

The winds outside are strong, with gusts from 25 to 30 miles per hour. As these winds whistle and whisk across his office window, he becomes even more jumpy at the sight of the shadows from the trees. At the slightest sound Teddy hears outside his office, he rushes out into the hallway, staring at the large wooden door at the end of hallway of the left wing. Teddy becomes afraid it might be time for his unwanted and dreadful meeting. Teddy is in agony; his nerves are just about shot from all this endless waiting. Teddy can't seem to make heads or tails of the stressful call he received late last evening. From the moment Teddy hung up the telephone, sleep escaped him. His mind seemed to be playing tricks on him, running in every direction, trying to figure out how things had gone so wrong and spiraled out of his control. Teddy was told to be prepared for a meeting this morning; he would have to answer some tough questions. The caller told him that for his sake, he'd better have the solutions. Frantically, he continues to pace back and forth, wringing his sweaty hands together.

After what seems a lifetime of waiting, the buzzer from the estate gate rings. Teddy quickly answers the buzzer before it alarms the staff. He doesn't want anyone to become aware of the secret meeting that was about to take place, whether he liked it or not. He tried not to sound nervous when asked who it was at the gate, even though he knew fully well who to expect that morning. Hearing the visitor's voice, Teddy quickly allowed the mysterious person onto the grounds of the Osbourne mansion. Teddy instructed the visitor to park in the parking lot near the entrance of the left wing. Then Teddy hurried down the long hallway to answer the door, making sure that no one else saw his visitor. Before the visitor could knock, Teddy snatched the door open, and once the visitor entered, Teddy quickly locked it. Then the two of them headed straight for Teddy's office. As soon as the two men walked into Teddy's office, they began shouting at one another. The visitor was blaming Teddy for something.

Unaware of anything out of the ordinary taking place at the mansion, Odessa wakes up to the song of a blue jay that lives in the tall tree just outside her bedroom window. Odessa's residence is located on the third floor in the left wing of the Osbourne mansion. Odessa lazily laid in bed for another 30 minutes with her eyes closed. Her bed was warm and cozy, and she was not quite ready to start her day. This morning was no different than any other morning, except Odessa awoke earlier than usual-- or so she thought. As Odessa laid there thinking over her daily routine, her alarm clock started to ring, informing her it was 6:45 a.m. It was officially time to start her day.

With her eyes still closed, Odessa turned towards her alarm to turn it off, simultaneously brushing some of her wavy brown hair out of her face. Odessa started removing the rest of her hair from her face, so she could open her large brown eyes to behold the new and promising day. Smiling, Odessa laid quietly for a few moments more in her comfortable and beautifully decorated, queen-size canopy bed. The sheets, pillow cases, comforter, and canopy drape all matched. They were white with a soft rose lace trim, and made from 800 count Egyptian cotton. Odessa loved soft colors; she felt they made her room bright and cozy. Odessa paused to give thanks to God; she felt blessed as she looked around her beautiful living quarters.

Not realizing how much time had gone by, Odessa sprang out of bed and walked across the room on her beautifully stained and well-varnished wood floors. Once she entered her private bathroom, Odessa brushed her pearly white teeth and then took her usual warm and cool shower. As soon as Odessa finished her shower, she dried herself off with a fluffy rose-colored towel that she took from her linen cabinet. After she was all dried off, Odessa hurriedly combed her hair and put on her uniform so she would be on time for work.

Odessa headed downstairs to perform all the daily duties as a live-in registered nurse. Odessa's employer and patient was Mr. Harrington Osbourne III. Odessa's job description, when hired, was to be a nurse for Mr. Osbourne. She affectionately addressed him as "Mr. O", with no disrespect intended on her part. As the years have passed, it would seem as though she had been hired to be his companion as well. After Mr. O has taken his meds at bedtime, he always finds a way to engage Odessa into some sort of conversation. Mr. O loved to have Odessa read to him, especially something from the Holy Bible. He knew full and well that between Odessa reading and his many questions, the whole thing would be drawn out until a quarter to nine. It was no surprise to Odessa that it took so long, seeing that was how Mr. O had planned it all along. Then and only then was Mr. O ready to retire for the evening.

Once Odessa left her room, she quickly closed the door behind her and headed for the stairwell. When she stepped into the stairwell, she quickly descended the mahogany spiral staircase. By the time

Odessa reached the landing between the second and first floor, she could hear voices coming from the foyer downstairs. At that time, Odessa couldn't make out who the voices belonged to. She could only determine from one of the high-pitched voices, that someone was very angry and upset. Odessa began to walk down the stairs slowly as she heard the voices getting louder and their footsteps quickly approaching in her direction. Odessa began to feel something was terribly wrong, so she quickly turned and ran quietly back to the landing.

Hiding out of sight, Odessa tried hard to listen to what was being said. She wanted to get some kind of answer as to why there were loud noises in the mansion, especially this early in the morning when everyone knew Geneva was still asleep. But by the time they approached the bottom of the stairs, where Odessa was hiding, their voices dropped to just a little above a whisper. Now that they were whispering, Odessa couldn't hear who was talking. So she quietly moved from her hiding place toward the edge of the stairs to see who was talking. She became very nervous upon seeing that it was Mr. O's son, Theodore Osbourne. He allowed some people to call him "Teddy." Odessa has never dreamed of calling him that. The other person Mr. Theodore was engaged in the angry conversation with, has his back turned toward the stairs. Odessa couldn't recognize him. She quickly realized there would be no time for breakfast; only a cup of coffee. The mysterious man was wearing a black hat and a long black coat. The man kept pointing his finger and making threatening hand gestures at Mr. Theodore. This made Odessa nervous and curious. Odessa desperately wanted to know who Mr. Theodore was talking to. Trying hard to see and hear what was going on, Odessa made a little noise, but she got out of sight as the mysterious stranger quickly turned in her direction. Odessa stayed back until she felt it was safe to look out again. She stepped out just in time to see who it was, and she got the shock of her life when she saw it was Mr. Markus Johns, the family's attorney. Instantly, questions began to flood Odessa's mind. "Why on earth was Mr. Johns at the mansion so early and what happened to cause Mr. Johns and Mr. Theodore to start shouting at each other? Why was Mr. Johns using his hands in such a threatening manner toward Mr. Theodore?"

Odessa knew she couldn't dare let them know she was trying to listen in on their conversation. After about fifteen more minutes had passed, Mr. Johns left.

Seizing the opportunity, Odessa decided to come downstairs, which created some noise. As soon as the startled Teddy heard the noise, he angrily looked up towards the top of the stairs. When Teddy realized that it was Odessa coming down the stairs, he immediately started questioning her. "Where are you coming from? Were you sneaking around and listening to my private conversation? I want to know what you heard. Tell me right now! Or I will have my father fire you in a moment's notice! I asked you a question Odessa, aren't you listening? Get your head out of the clouds and answer me this instant," Teddy demanded.

Finally, Teddy stopped talking as Odessa approached him and stood on the bottom step. Odessa answered Mr. Theodore with a puzzled look on her face. "First of all, I would like to understand why are you shouting at me first thing in the morning. Has something or someone upset you? And furthermore, what are you talking about?"

Then Teddy started speaking to Odessa in a harsh, but lowered voice. "Odessa, don't answer my question with a question! And Odessa, where are you on your way to anyway?" Odessa answered Teddy again with another question: "Where do you think I'm going, Mr. Theodore?" Then, just as quickly as she had asked Teddy the question, Odessa answered it for him. "Well if you must know, I'm on my way to work in the right wing to take care of your father. Isn't that what I'm being paid for, Mr. Theodore?" Teddy was so mad, he turned even redder than he already was and shouted at Odessa again. "Then why are you still here? Odessa, we aren't paying you to just stand around and talk, so get moving." With that, Odessa took her cue and went down the hall to the right wing.

CHAPTER

2

ODESSA RUSHED DOWN THE long hallway, trying to make up some lost time. Odessa headed straight for the drawing room to see Mr. O. The drawing room was very large, yet warm and inviting. In the mornings, Mr. O spent a lot of time in the drawing room. In the afternoons, he spent most of his time in the library. That was a part of Mr. Osbourne's daily routines. No sooner than Odessa entered the drawing room, Mr. O started joking with her. He asked, "Odessa what happened to you this morning? You're twenty-five minutes late, hun." With a grin on his face, he said, "You must've had a long night." Odessa responded by saying, "Ah, I see someone has gotten up on the right side of the bed." Then Odessa proceeded to take Mr. O's vitals. She placed the stethoscope on his chest and back; instructing him to breathe in and out. Odessa tried to listen to his lungs to see if they were clearing up. Mr. O has had a cough from a nasty cold, which has lasted much longer than expected.

Odessa is kind of concerned about it, although she would never let Mr. O see her concern. The doctor had asked her to keep a close watch on the cough. The doctor felt that if they weren't careful, it could turn into pneumonia. Once Odessa was finished with Mr. O's morning vitals, she administered his meds. Mr. O didn't require constant care. Most days, Odessa just made sure Mr. O had eaten so that he could take his meds and checked his IV line to make sure it was still open and flowing properly. Mr. O is scheduled to take his meds three times a day: mornings between eight and eight-thirty, noon, and just before bed at about seven-thirty.

Mr. O questioned Odessa to see if she had heard some loud talking this morning, about a quarter past eight. Odessa didn't respond to Mr. O's question at first, because she didn't really want to. Odessa didn't know how to answer his question; she didn't know what happened between Mr. Theodore and Mr. Johns. Then Mr. O asked another question along the same line as his first one. "Odessa, do you know who was making all that racket early this morning, and what for?" Mr. O was looking to Odessa for information. Since she wasn't able to give him any information, she answered him with a "yes," by nodding her head up and down. Odessa knew that she couldn't tell Mr. O everything. Odessa only said she had heard voices and someone leaving out of the left-wing side door.

That was a side entrance and exit to the side driveway and parking lot. The Osbournes built the driveway and parking lot on the property after Rebecca and her husband, Freddrick's sudden deaths. It was a type of memorial to them. Rebecca and Freddrick died in an automobile accident, but Geneva had somehow survived with help from a stranger.

That fatal day was Rebecca and Freddrick's eleventh anniversary. They had planned the vacation months ahead of time, juggling their schedules so they would be able take their only child, Geneva, with them. They wanted to spend time celebrating their anniversary, as well as some quality family time together. They planned on having lots of fun and some much-needed relaxation. But before they were able to start their vacation, they had one important obligation to fulfill. Rebecca and Freddrick were to meet with Mr. Johns to drop off and sign some papers that Mr. O had Mr. Johns draw up for him. Unfortunately, before they were able to do so, they both perished in a car accident. Odessa only knew this because Mr. O had confided in her about it. Whenever Mr. O brought up the day that Rebecca and Freddrick died, he would become sad and very upset. He would recite the same words over and over, to the letter, claiming he would go to his grave, believing that it was never an accident. He would repeat these words with a broken heart and spirit: *"I believe they have been murdered."*

As in times past, Mr. O confided in Odessa about his thoughts of Rebecca's death, telling Odessa that she reminded him so much of his beloved Rebecca. He said she was just as kind and as free-spirited as Rebecca was, and that he was going to remember her in his will. Each time after Mr. O said this out loud, there was a change in him; for just an instant, you could see all the hurt and pain of Rebecca's death in his face. Sadly, just as Mr. O had done in past times, he'd turn away, so Odessa wouldn't see the tears streaming down his face. Then Mr. O said in a very low, soft tone, "It's been ten long years, and I still don't know everything that happened or why."

CHAPTER

3

ODESSA DIDN'T KNOW EVERYTHING about Geneva, yet she somehow felt close to her. But for some reason, Geneva didn't particularly care for Odessa. Geneva would often make remarks like, "You will never take my mother's place!" As if Odessa had ever tried or wanted to! Odessa felt a strange sense of closeness with Geneva, maybe because she also lost her mother at an early age.

Right then and there, Odessa's mind traveled back to the time when she first heard of her mother's fatal illness:

It was a very cold and dark fall night, when I awoke from a deep sleep to many voices, and one was louder than all the others. At the time, I was only five years old, and couldn't understand what the person was shouting about or why were they so upset, but I knew he had caused me to abruptly wake up. I called out to my mommy, but there was no answer. So I cried out with an even louder voice, "Mommy!" Then I heard a loud thump, and I saw Aunt Greta coming up the stairs. Aunt Greta was mommy's sister; she was always at their house since mommy became ill. Aunt Greta told me to go back to bed and assured me that everything was alright. But somehow, even at five years of age, I knew everything wasn't alright, and it would never be alright again.

Earlier that day, as I sat and played on the floor in our country-styled kitchen, mommy baked cookies. She always busied herself, throughout the years, with baking cakes, pies, and cookies for family gatherings. I said "Mmm, cookies; they smell so good!" I could tell by the smell, that mommy was cooking two of my favorite cookies: chocolate chip and lemon drop. I knew that mommy would give me some cookies right out of the oven, but not before they had cooled off. The phone rang, distracting mommy. After the phone rang again, she wiped her hands off on her apron and answered the phone. "Hello... Yes, this is she... no... no... it's not so." Some time had passed since mommy's phone call had ended; she was in what I now know to be a daze. I called to her several times, but she acted as if she didn't hear me. Then I yelled louder, as I pulled desperately at mommy's apron, trying to tell her the stove was smoking. Startled, she snatched open the oven. Right away, the kitchen was filled with lots of smoke. Mommy, realizing I was still sitting at the kitchen table, told me to go upstairs right away so I wouldn't breathe all that smoke into my lungs. As I was running out of the kitchen, I saw mommy rush to open the kitchen doors and windows to let the smoke out. Well, you can see that I didn't get any cookies. I just fell asleep for the night.

Later that evening, dad came home from working at the office, The Preston Lumber Mill, which had been in his family forever.

Every year my father's company would clear a portion of the lumber yard to have a big family reunion. Everyone would dress up, but only the children who were 13 and older were allowed to attend it. The rest of the children, 12 and under, were left behind to have a sleepover at a designated cousin's house. The following day after the family reunion, our family always had a really big picnic, and everyone was invited-- even us younger kids. The menu would always consist of barbeque ribs, chicken, hot dogs, hamburgers, potato salad, chips, and lots of other good food and desserts. Everyone was encouraged to play games. Softball was always a big hit at these picnics. Afterwards, we told tall tales about who the best player was, and who got the most hits and home runs. But after all the tall tales, everyone came out to these outings just to have fun.

When I woke up, it was Saturday morning. I went down to breakfast as I always did-- in my pajamas. We would eat all kinds of good stuff for breakfast on Saturdays. We would eat eggs, bacon, and chocolate chip pancakes with faces. They also served hot maple syrup and fresh-squeezed orange juice. The orange juice was my favorite. Dad always said mommy was the best cook; much better than all her sisters, and just the best cook in the whole darn county. Mommy would always smile every time dad said that. But today she wasn't there to smile or get on him about drinking so much coffee before the meal and ruining his appetite. (Dad's response would always be, "Ruth, since when have I ever been so full of coffee that I couldn't stuff myself with your good cooking?") But this wasn't the case today-- when I reached the bottom of the stairs I had heard someone say "hush." So I slowly entered the living room, remembering that I was taught never to run in the house-- especially that particular room.

As I got closer to dad's high back lounging chair, he scooped me up in his arms. I began to look around the room for mom, but all I saw was a lot of my aunts and uncles. They were all either speaking in quiet voices, or staring in our direction. Mommy wasn't in her usual chair, the rocking chair I had given mommy on her last birth-day. That rocking chair never matched one thing in that room; yet mommy put it in there anyway because dad and I bought it for her. That's where Mommy usually sat and knitted all kinds of stuff. She loved cooking, baking, knitting and making all sorts of crafts, and she helped me make my dad's first father's day gift when I was only two. Mommy also helped me make a picture frame, and now here it sits in this room with a picture of the three of us. I had forgotten to say good morning to everyone-- I just blurted out "Where is mommy?"

Before anyone could answer, I shouted "Why hasn't mommy made breakfast for us?" Then I said in an even louder voice "Daddy, where is mommy?" as I was trying to climb down from his lap. Dad pulled me closer to him and began rubbing my head. He said, "Odessa, sit here with me I want tell you something." My Aunt Heather began to cry, and then I asked my daddy, "where is Mommy?" He held me close and said Mommy had an accident and she was in the hospital. I told my dad to take me to mommy right away, she needs me, and I have to take care of her like she does me when I'm sick. There was a knock at the door, and Uncle Vick answered to find more aunts, uncles and cousins from both sides of our family. But, I wasn't interested in them; I was still telling daddy we had to get ready so we could go and take care of mommy.

My Aunt Heather said she would go upstairs and help me get ready, so we went upstairs and I began asking her all kinds of questions about my mom, and how she got hurt in the accident. Aunt Heather never said anything, but I noticed that she kept her head turned away from me. Then I asked her where mommy was hurt, and what did she think I needed to take to help her feel better. But Aunt Heather never said what to take, and she definitely never said how mommy got into an accident or even where she was hurt. I told my Aunt Heather that we have a 'heart a kit', it was a box that me and mommy had made together to take care of all kinds of boo boo's with lots of love. Then she said I could take the whole box, so we would have everything that we would need to fix mommy and make her all better.

Aunt Alice came upstairs, while Aunt Heather was getting me ready and putting blue ribbons on my braids. Aunt Heather had braided my hair just like mommy did, in two big braids. I always enjoyed it when Aunt Heather helped me get dressed, because she always treated me like a big girl just like mommy always did. Aunt Alice asked Aunt Heather to step out into the hallway for a moment, and when she did, I heard Aunt Heather say "No, no, no!" Aunt Alice spoke up and said, "You have to be quiet and get yourself together for Odessa and Bruce." That's my daddy's name; he was named after Grandpa Bruce. When I heard Aunt Heather say that last "no," I ran into the hallway and demanded to know what was wrong. And how much longer would it be before we left to go see mommy? We have to go soon so mommy can get better and come home.

My darkest moment was in the hallway while I was trying to find answers. I looked up, and daddy had just reached the top of the stairs. With tears in his eyes he grabbed me and said, "Baby it's over, it's over. Mommy has gone to live in that big pie in the sky. You know she is with your grandparents now, and they are all having a reunion at this very moment." He was trembling, and I was trying with all my strength to pull out of his grip, but he held me even tighter and closer. Daddy looked into my eyes as the tears fell from his, and he said "It's just the two us now, just me and you, Odessa." I told Daddy "no, it's three of us: you, mommy and me, and we have to go help mommy, because we don't want her to stay at the reunion with them. Hurry daddy, we have to go take care of mommy, okay?" Daddy said, "no, mommy is gone forever; she went to live with God. You know how mommy always said, 'that is where you go when you leave here, and sleep forever, and then you wake there?' Mommy went to sleep here, and woke up in heaven." I began to cry and scream "I want my mommy back!"

There was a funeral but I wasn't allowed to go-- everyone felt it would be too hard for me to deal with and they didn't want me to have bad dreams. Our neighbor, Mrs. Poke stayed with me during mommy's funeral services at Morning Glory Baptist Church-- our family church-- and I didn't get a chance to say goodbye, mommy.

Odessa was still in deep thoughts from her past, when she heard Mr. O calling her name. Apparently he had been calling Odessa for sometime. Once he knew he had her attention again he said, "I guess I lost you there for a few moments." Odessa hurriedly apologized, "I'm sorry Mr. O, I guess I was in deep thoughts there for a moment or two."

"I would say so," answered Mr. O, "perhaps a dime for your thoughts, seeing that inflation is going up!" They both laughed. Mr. O asked Odessa if she still had those papers that he had asked her to hide somewhere no one could ever find them. Not waiting for a response, Mr. O asked, "You did put them away?" Mr. O seemed kind of nervous and very serious. Odessa asked Mr. O if anything was wrong, and was there anything that she could help him with? She saw that he was getting upset because he was coughing even more today than ever, and trying harder to catch his breath.

Odessa hooked him up to the oxygen tank so he could breathe more easily. After a half hour or so, he started to breathe better. Odessa was more concerned now than ever about Mr. O, so she tried calling the doctor, to no avail. She left a message for him to "come see Mr. Osbourne as soon as possible, because he's having difficulty breathing." Odessa whispered into the telephone, "and please hurry!"

After she hung up the phone, Mr. O asked her to have Oscar to bring him a cup of tea, as Mr. O said it always makes him feel better when he drinks warm tea. He asked Odessa to join him, but she declined. "Well I guess I have to drink alone." Mr. O laughed so hard until he began coughing even more.

After that episode of coughing passed, she decided it would be a good thing to take Mr. O vitals again. She didn't like the readings. Mr. O's pulse rate was faster than it was earlier, and his pressure was higher. Odessa took notice as Mr. O started sipping his tea, that it seemed to have calmed him down.

Mr. O told Odessa there are going to be some big changes around here come tomorrow. "I'm going to make them while I'm still alive and able to do so. I'm not going to leave nothing to chance; I will make these changes while I still have breath in this old body." He didn't laugh this time, so Odessa knew he was serious. But what was Mr. O so serious about? What kind of changes was he talking about? She was about to ask him when Oscar showed up and said his lunch was ready to be served in the library as per his request during breakfast this morning. Mr. O asked Odessa if she was going to eat her lunch, since he knew she hadn't had breakfast. "Of course!" she replied, "Maybe I'll eat with you in the library." She hoped she could get some insight as to what he was talking about or what was bothering him that got him all upset. Mr. O responded, "You will do no such thing!" Laughingly, he instructed Odessa to go and enjoy her lunch and that he would see her afterwards. He looked back at Oscar, saying "Move this chair. I have to eat and discuss some important business. We need to go over some notes from last evening at the same time." Then turning again to Odessa, he smiled, "I will see you after lunch young lady."

CHAPTER

4

ALL THROUGH LUNCH ODESSA has been wondering what, or who, has Mr. O so upset? What was all that craziness with Mr. Theodore and Mr. Johns earlier that morning? Odessa also started to reflect back on how Mr. Theodore was threatening her earlier as well. While these thoughts raced through her mind, she took the last bite of lasagna and lunch was finally over. She took off in the direction of the library, located in the left wing.

The left wing was very nice and cozy. Its upper two floors were set up mostly as guest quarters. Odessa has been residing in a large suite on the third floor since she was hired eight years ago by her boss, Mr. Harrington Osbourne III. On the weekends she stays at an apartment on north side of Chicago in the Bryn Mawr Historic District. Odessa loves that area of the city, with its varieties of commerce and stately structures. She shares the two bedroom apartment with her best friend Lisa Taylor. She and Lisa have been friends since the seventh grade, and were inseparable all thru high school. They even went to the same college. Both were in the medical field—Odessa became a registered nurse, and Lisa, after achieving her M.A. in business, works as the assistant director of medical/ billing records. Before Odessa went to work for Mr. O, she and Lisa both worked at Northwestern Hospital.

Finally, Odessa arrived at the library, pausing a moment before entering to hear what sounded like laughter from inside. She decided to knock as she entered the library, and that's when she saw Geneva hugging her grandfather from behind. Both of them looked and sounded very happy, but there was something in Geneva's eyes as she turned to look Odessa's direction. It was as if she had caught Geneva's hands in the cookie jar. Her mouth was making laughing sounds, but her eyes were different; they were an unnerving kind of cold. It made Odessa feel a flash of sickness in the pit of her stomach, which lasted for a fleeting moment. Odessa took notice of that eerie feeling, and the movement of Geneva's hands. It was the same way she always hugged Mr. O, but now it seemed a bit strange. Maybe she was just a little paranoid since her talk with Mr. O, and the statements he had made before lunch. Why was he making all these new changes, and in such a fireball hurry? Mr. O looked as if he was having a good time with Geneva, but after Odessa came in she started getting ready to leave. "If I didn't know any better," Odessa thought, "I'd think she was in a hurry to leave us alone in the library." In a way, she was glad Geneva left so she could ask Mr. O what he was talking about earlier.

Before she could give Mr. O his meds or take his vitals, he asked her to go to the other side of the room to get a book for him. On her way to retrieve it, Odessa heard him say, "I can't breathe," and she turned to see him grabbing his chest. She ran toward Mr. O, asking him at the same time "what's wrong?" Just that fast, Mr. O slumped over before she could reach him. Odessa started administering CPR, while hollering for someone to help. Oscar arrived and asked, "what happened here?" Odessa didn't speak right away because she was trying her hardest to save Mr. O. Oscar asked what he could do to help. Odessa could barely get it out, but she told him to call 911 and ask them to send an ambulance, and to "please hurry! Mr. O is coding"! Odessa was still trying to breathe for Mr. O. Somehow, during the course of starting the CPR on him, she felt a sticky substance on his chest which in turn got on her fingers. There was no time to wipe it off her hands; she couldn't think about that. All her thoughts and actions were directed at saving her friend, whose life which was now hanging in the balance. The paramedics arrived about six minutes later with a lot of equipment; they asked Odessa to step back and let them take over took over administering CPR. Three minutes into it one of them shook his head, it was to no avail-- Mr. O was gone.

Just when Odessa thought her day couldn't get any worse, Teddy entered the library, with three Evanston police officers in tow, accusing Odessa of murdering his father. Teddy was shouting, "and after everything my father has done for Odessa and her church, this is the way she repays him!" Teddy disliked and disapproved of Odessa from day one; maybe he thought this was his one and only chance to make her pay. "You all know Odessa murdered my father because he cut her out of his will." Teddy continued shouting and spitting at the top of his voice, like a caged animal foaming at the mouth. "I told my father to get rid of her! Arrest her! Arrest her! Handcuff Odessa right now! I tell you she is the only one who could have murdered him! She planned it! Can't you see my poor father lying there; dead! Odessa executed her plan well didn't she? I tell you she won't get away with it; I won't let her! I want Odessa prosecuted to the fullest extent of the law!" Teddy was ranting and raving terribly. He had to make sure he kept throwing out as many bad things about Odessa as possible, to make her not only look guilty but to be guilty.

"How could Mr. Theodore say such a thing about me?" Odessa thought to herself. "He knew that me and his father were friends."

Teddy had never felt safe or secure of his place in his father's eyes or heart. Nor had he ever sensed or felt that his father loved him like the love and affection he would always display with Rebecca his sister, or Geneva his niece. Teddy never knew how to get that which he wanted from his father. Now there was someone else in the picture he had to compete with, and she wasn't even family. How much more of this could he stand or must he take? It was that dreadful Odessa, his father's nurse-- or so she pretends to be. Teddy had built up a serious hatred for Odessa and he hides it well, or so he thinks anyway. Now he feels that she has stolen enough from him. Not only has she taken his father's love and affection, but she is also a stranger and outsider, a Christian freak. "And God knows what else she was doing to or with my father," Teddy thought. "But not today-- she's going away for a very long time and I will make sure she does. That's why I told everyone that she murdered my father!"

Odessa was just standing there, in shock and bewildered, upset and broken hearted at the death of her friend and employer. She was asking herself "why is Mr. Theodore saying all these horrible things about me?" He knows she wouldn't ever have tried to harm Mr. O-- they were friends. He had to know this because Mr. O told everyone in the house at least one time or another. Odessa began to cry as they started to put Mr. O onto the stretcher, and placed the sheet over his head. Mr. Theodore jumped right in, saying "why are you crying? I know why, because you have been caught in your own trap." Officer Mickey from the Evanston police department told Teddy to calm down, and said he would ask the questions. At this point, Teddy was still shouting and making even more accusations. Officer Mickey asked Odessa to tell him, in her own words, what happened here today. She was still sobbing and in shock, and focused on paramedics as they were removing Mr. O's body from the library. Odessa didn't really hear or understand what the officer had said, or whether or not he was talking to her or someone else in the room. Officer Mickey noticed Odessa was in a state of shock, so he asked Oscar to get her something cool to drink, and asked Odessa to sit down. Teddy shouted, "sit down? I want her out of here, why haven't you arrested her yet? My father is dead and now you're asking her to have a seat. Get her out of here; she killed him, and I'm already about to take matters into my own hands. If you don't hurry up and get Odessa out of our home; I'll have your badge for this!"

Shortly into the interview with Odessa, Detective Brad Rodgers entered the library and immediately asked, "is this a crime scene?" Officer Mickey nodded yes, then Det. Rogers asked the officer "then why haven't you taped it off? What are you doing that is so darn important, that it isn't taped off. And for heaven sake why are all these people walking around and tampering with my evidence? If any of my evidence is tainted, I will not be a happy camper!" He told the other officers "please get all these people out of here, except for the nurse-- I want to talk to her alone. Teddy started to shout again: "if she's staying I'm staying." Det. Rodgers asked the officer who was the closest to him, "who is that guy that's making all that noise in here?

The officer replied "he's the son of the deceased, and he's accusing his father's nurse of murder."

Det. Rodgers addressed the other officers on duty. "Didn't I say clear this room? You take everyone out of here into another room and wait for my instructions. I don't take kindly to people doing their own thing. I also don't like when you're not following my orders or protocol, have I made myself clear? Now clear this room immediately!" Then he turned to Odessa, who was sitting down in a corner chair in the library, "are you feeling better?" Oscar had just given her some water to drink. Det. Rodgers introduced himself to Odessa, and told her he would like to ask her a few questions about what happened in the library between her and Mr. Osbourne before he died. Odessa started to explain, but began to cry all over again. He placed his hand on her shoulder and told her to take her time, as he continued taking notes.

Odessa said when she arrived to the library after lunch that she heard laughter coming from inside the library. She said she paused for a moment then she knocked on the door before entering. When she came in she saw Mr. O, "that's what I affectionately called him. He was over at his desk and he and his granddaughter Geneva were laughing. Geneva was hugging him from behind and rubbing his chest the way she always does. Then she left the room, and Mr. O asked me to get a book from over there," as she pointed in the direction of the book he had asked for. "I walked over to get the book and Mr. O stated that he couldn't breathe. I rushed over to him, but he was already slumping over. I started administering CPR right away. In between giving him CPR I called out for someone help and to call 911. Oscar came in and asked what was wrong? I told him to call 911 and inform them that Mr. O isn't breathing. He called while I kept trying to breathe for Mr. O, I was doing all that I've been trained to do, to try and save his life. When the paramedics arrived they took over, performing CPR, until they said he was gone. Right after that, Mr. Theodore came in with your officers, accusing me of murdering Mr. O." Then Odessa said in a real soft voice, with tears streaming down her face, "he wasn't just my employer, he was my friend, and we were friends."

While Det. Rogers was observing Odessa's reactions to Teddy's accusations, he noticed she kept rubbing her fingers together as if she had something on them. He asked her about it, and she said "it came off Mr. O's chest when I began to administer CPR. I know that it wasn't anything on my hand before this happened." He asked if she minded if he took a sample of it, and she said she didn't because she had nothing to hide. Det. Rogers had another officer collect the sample and take it directly to the lab. Odessa continued talking to him, stating she would do whatever it takes to help find out what happened to her dear Mr. O. Once the officer said he had the sample, Det. Rodgers told him to tell the lab he wanted the results yesterday.

Officer Mickey and the other officer were conducting interviews and taking notes from the rest of the household, including from Teddy. Teddy was still spreading lies about Odessa. Right then, an officer walked over to Det. Rodgers and whispered something in his ear, but Odessa wasn't able to hear. She began thinking "that is the second time this has happened to me today." Just then Det. Rodgers excused himself, instructing Odessa to sit tight and he would be right back.

Det. Rogers came back after about an hour, and told Odessa that they were taking her to the station, for further questioning. They didn't allow her take any of her belongings; they just put her in the car and drove directly to the Evanston police station on Howard Street.

CHAPTER

5

UPON HER ARRIVAL AT the police station, Odessa was placed in a small interrogation room, with windows that were high up and very close to the ceiling. The walls were painted a greenish blue, and the floors were tiled with dark brown twelve by twelve commercial tiles. The room had one long table with three dirty white chairs pushed under it. Odessa was asked to sit down and get comfortable in one of the chairs, and they would be right with her. While sitting in that room alone, Odessa began to let her mind drift back on the events of the day. Out of nowhere, she saw Geneva's eyes again. She did not understand what it meant, only that she felt that same old eerie feeling she felt when she saw Geneva in the library after lunch. What was it about her eyes? Odessa was deep in thought, as she began to ponder about Geneva's eyes. Maybe it was something she had missed or forgotten. She was so deep in thought that she didn't hear the detective come back into room.

After the second time they had questioned her, Det. Rodgers left the room to order search warrants, both for her room at the Osbourne's mansion and her apartment in the city.

Another Officer entered the room, and he began to interrogate Odessa all over again for the third time. She gave him the same answers she had given before at the Osbourne's mansion. Her story was the truth and she never changed it. He asked her if she knew of anyone in the house who would want to do any harm to her employer. She said she didn't know of anyone that would want to harm Mr. O.

Later Odessa remembered she hadn't told anyone about the conversation she and Mr. O were having before Oscar showed up to take him to lunch in the library. Now this officer was asking her, "so what were you and Mr. O talking about?" Odessa wasn't sure if she should or could tell anyone about that last conversation that they had. Not really knowing what to say about it, Odessa looked at the officer and said she didn't know, stating that it was mainly Mr. O doing the most of the talking. Odessa said, "during lunch I decided that I would bring up the discussion again when I went to give Mr. O his afternoon meds. As fate would have it, I never had a chance to find out what it was really all about. I wish I could try and figure out what Mr. O meant by the big changes he was going to make tomorrow."

Once Det. Rodgers reentered the room, he walked over to Odessa. He started off by saying he was sorry, but they were placing her under arrest for the murder of Mr. Harrington Osbourne III, and then had the officer Mirandize her. After reading her her rights, the officer took Odessa to booking. The booking officer took Odessa's fingerprints and her picture. After about five hours at this station, they transferred her by car to the Cook County Jail at 26th and California in Chicago, for a bond hearing that would take place the following day. Odessa was visibly upset, and she continued declaring to all those in whom she came in contact with that she was innocent. Before placing her in a cell, she was allowed her one phone call. Odessa was so upset, she couldn't remember her dad's phone number, so she called her pastor, Pastor Mike Trust.

Pastor Mike had been her pastor since she was born, and he baptized her as a little girl. Every Sunday he gives great sermons, but Wednesday nights his teachings are out of this world, and Odessa has learned so much from him. The day she accepted Christ into her life as Lord and Savior, it was on one of those Wednesday nights. He was teaching from the Holy Bible on the book of Romans. More recently, Pastor Mike has been coming by to drop off tapes for Odessa. These tapes were from the Wednesday nights services, since she hadn't been able to attend them since she came to work for Mr. O.

One day while he was dropping off some tapes to Odessa, he met Mr. O. They had a great time talking together, and Mr. O asked him a lot of questions about their church. Odessa had told him previously they were having a building drive. Mr. O laughed and said, "May I inquirer as to where will the building be driving off to?" This caused Pastor Mike, as Odessa calls him, to laugh as well. So, he explained that their church is very old and in need of some very large repairs, that cost a lot of money. Mr. O interjected, "you have a large congregation, right? This is what Odessa has been telling me. So, why doesn't the church have money for the repairs?" Pastor Mike explained there are a lot of people out of work and struggling, trying to make it. "The church tries to help the families in need as much as we can, and that takes away from the reserves. So, after all is said and done, there is not much money left for repairs." Mr. O looked up over his glasses as he was saying "we will have none of that! The church must be fixed so my friend Odessa can keep learning. Then she can return with even more great stories from the Bible, and share them with me. I so enjoy our evenings together when she reads to me from the Bible. She reads with such joy and enthusiasm. Most evenings I can hardly wait until it is my bedtime. I always get her to stay longer with some form of excuse so we can talk or she can read to me until I get really sleepy, usually at a quarter to nine. And when you drop by next week, stop in to see me, Ok?"

The following week Mr. O invited both Pastor Mike and Odessa to the library to have a cup of tea with him. Mr. O told them that he had sat up a trust fund to help the church, and not just to repair the existing church, but there was enough to build a new one as well. Also in the trust, Mr. O had purchased six acres of land to build it on. When he gave it to Pastor Mike, he told him he wanted to give back to the place that had helped Odessa to become so kind, caring, and sweet. He told Pastor Mike "most of all Odessa is so sincere, and so loving toward her fellow man. Odessa constantly reminds me so much of my late daughter, Rebecca." With that he told Odessa and Pastor Mike that he had to get back to work, so they both left.

Odessa knew why he had asked them to leave-- often Mr. O would become sad at the very mention of Rebecca's name.

Back in her cell, Odessa still couldn't believe what was happening to her. She started to cry and feel sorry for herself, saying "someone has to realize that I'm not capable of murder. What kind of evidence do they have against me? Was it all because of Mr. Theodore and his accusations toward me?" However, knowing that they didn't believe her she asked herself: what's next? Who could she trust? Who would listen? Everything was moving so fast Odessa just couldn't seem to grasp what was going on, much less understand why it was happening to her.

She began to pray and ask God for His guidance and protection, and to please intervene on her behalf. Once again she saw Geneva's eyes. Why was she seeing them? She didn't understand why, she just knew it had to mean something, but what? Odessa continued to try and make heads or tails about what happened to Mr. O, but to no avail. "Why were they saying he was murdered? Wasn't it a heart attack? He said that he couldn't breathe, and he was grabbing hold of the front of his shirt. That's how he was when I reached him, holding it and slumped over. I did all I knew to do so, why is it murder?"

CHAPTER

6

WHILE SHE WAS SEARCHING her mind for answers, the guard on duty came in to tell her that she had a visitor in the waiting room. He told her to step forward and turn around with her back to him, so he could place the handcuffs on her. Then he led her down the hall to the waiting room where she met Mr. Barry Straitway for the very first time. Mr. Straitway has been an attorney for seventeen years. He's married to his college sweetheart, Mae Helen. They've been married for eighteen years. They married the year before he passed the Bar. Mae Helen, is a saved Christian woman who loves the Lord, and very active in their church. Barry attends church services on Sunday mornings just to appease his wife. She's always after him to accept Jesus as his Lord and Savior; she says she wants him to go Heaven when he dies. His response to that is always the same: he's got too much living to do to even think about dying. As of yet, he hasn't accepted Christ as part of his life. He was always worried if one of his colleagues found out he was a Christian. "Finding that out about me wouldn't be so bad," he thought, "but what would happen if they discovered that I'm not only a Christian but a saved one, a real holy roller! That would ruin any chances that I may have to be appointed to the bench. I should just hand them the hammer and nails to seal my career in a coffin. I'll never have my dream of becoming a judge come to pass!"

Earlier that evening, while sitting down to dinner with Mae Helen, he received the call concerning Odessa. Pastor Trust asked him if he would be willing to take her case. Everyone around town knew of his reputation in and out of the courtroom. After their conversation, he hung up the telephone, then placed a call to the courthouse. He asked the officer who answered a few questions about who might be handling the prosecution side of the case. The officer replied that he heard through the courthouse grapevine Prosecutor Prod had already assigned it to himself. After hanging up, he looked kind of puzzled as he headed back to sit down at the dinner table. Mae Helen was watching his expressions all the time he was on the phone, and she knew that he was bothered by something that he had heard. So she jokingly asked him, "What's wrong? Did you lose your bowling match?" He began to confide in Mae Helen about his concerns, and that he may not have a chance to win the case. With all the evidence that is stacked up against this girl, they seem as though they're not just trying Odessa for Mr. Osbourne's murder, but for her faith and who she believes. Mr. Prod is known to go after anyone who confesses salvation. Besides he always wins: he has never, in his career, lost one case. "Who do I think I am fooling? This trial is already fixed! The deck is already stacked against her. I bet they're already planning their horse and pony show. I've told you before how Mr. Prod likes bringing his theatrics into the courtroom. He's probably, right at this very moment, trying her in the public's eyes. He has won and we have lost, before our side can even hope of finding-- much less interviewing or cross examining-- one witness. Mr. Prod will try and turn this trial into a circus. He's the one who tries to make Christians out to be clowns, and just all around big jokes." Mae Helen interrupted, explaining to him "when it's all said and done GOD has the last word, neither Mr. Prod nor the Judge has final say. They just need Christ in their life, and you need him too!" Then she tried calming him down by telling him how great of an attorney he was, and for him to use all the resources that he had at his disposal. "And don't forget to let Doris do her job."

Doris Pickles is Mr. Straitway's assistant and investigator, and is really good at what she does. When she's on an assignment, she's like a hungry dog that gets hold of a bone with just a little piece of meat on it, she sucks it dry. That's the way she goes after evidence for a case. She's just like Mr. Prod, she never quits without turning over every stone to make sure she finds what she is looking for. If it's there she will find it-- that's the reason Mr. Prod tried to hire her out from under Mr. Straitway. He offered her a big fat salary, but she told him she was happy right where she was. Mr. Prod has had it in for her ever since. Doris believes in Odessa's innocence, and come hell or high water she's determined to help her get set free from the jaws of Mr. Prod.

Once the guard removed the cuffs from Odessa's wrists, he left them alone. Mr. Straitway explained to Odessa that he had been hired to be her attorney. She asked him by whom? Mr. Straitway told Odessa that he was hired by her Pastor and her church to defend her in this matter.

Mr. Straitway asked Odessa if anyone had read her Miranda rights to her. She didn't quite understand the question, and he saw this in her face before she could say anything. So Mr. Straitway rephrased the question: "Odessa did they read you your rights when they placed you under arrest?" Odessa nodded yes, and asked "Mr. Straitway why, did they arrest me? I haven't done anything. You have to believe me, I'm innocent!" Mr. Straitway explained that it didn't matter to him whether or not Odessa was guilty or innocent; he just had to provide her with the best defense possible.

Mr. Straitway told Odessa that from where he was standing the case isn't really looking good for her. "How 'bout we start from the very beginning, because that prosecutor that has taken this case against you will leave no stones unturned. The Prosecutor's office feels that they have enough evidence stacked up against you; Mr. Prod is already talking about the death penalty. There's talk that after this case, Mr. Prod is dead set on running for some bigger political office using you as his stepping stone to get there. So, whether I believe you or not, this is a very big case-- one of the biggest of all time. Everyone is already talking and trying to predict its outcome. It is very political as well, it one that will make or break careers.

"They are accusing you of murdering a very wealthy and power-ful businessman. The news around the circuit is that Mr. Harrington Osbourne was very influential, and had a lot of connections in high places. Now Odessa, it is time for you to take your seat; for you and I are about to embark on a very adventurous roller coaster ride, with all its highs and lows." Odessa's eyes got as big as saucers, and she said "can Mr. Prod really do that?" Mr. Straitway answered Odessa "yes, and they already have." "Oh my God, I haven't done anything, why is this happening? It is like I'm having a bad dream-- really a nightmare-- that I just can't seem to wake up from." Right away Mr. Straitway interjected, "you are not having a nightmare, but you are about to live one."

"Now Odessa, as I was saying, starting from your first recollec-tion of today's events, tell me what happened. Try not to leave out any details, however obsolete you may think something is, Odessa you must tell me everything that you can remember. It will at the very least help me to help you. This will help tell me the way your mind works under pressure and stress. First I need you to relax and give me your best recall of all the events of the day thru your *mind's* eyes. I need to see what you saw-- this in and of itself will help me determine the best way to handle your defense."

Odessa took a deep breath, and started from what she believed was the beginning, her first memory of the day. She said "once I left my room, and started down the long spiral stairs. They are a few steps away from my bedroom door. Once I started down the stairs, I began hearing what I felt were at least two loud voices, one a little louder and angrier than the other." Odessa said she didn't know what all the hollering was about, but she did manage to see who it was. "It was Mr. Theodore-- he is Mr. Osbourne's son-- and Mr. Johns the family's attorney." Odessa told Mr. Straitway that she'd heard them coming toward her direction, so she quietly ran back up to the top of the stairs and was hidden out of sight. "That was how I was able to see them but they didn't see me."

"After Mr. Johns' left, exiting out the left wing door, I decided it would be a good time to try and go downstairs, to go to work. I felt if I made some noise as I came down the stairs, it wouldn't look suspicious to Mr. Theodore. But, as soon as he heard me on the stairs, he turned in my direction. When he looked up and saw it was me, Mr. Theodore immediately started accusing me of sneaking around and trying to hear his private conversations. He ordered me to tell him what he wanted to know, stating if I didn't tell him what he felt I might have heard he threatened that he would have his father to fire me. I really never heard anything that I could understand. Mr. Theodore and Mr. Johns were shouting from a distance, but as they were approaching the bottom of the stairs their voices dropped, just a little above a whisper. When Mr. Theodore asked me again what had I heard, I told him once again that I had heard nothing. Feeling satisfied with my answers, and that I really hadn't heard anything, Mr. Theodore ordered me to go to work-- but not before telling me that he'll be watching me and that they weren't paying me to just stand around.

Odessa paused for a moment, then she continued. "I arrived to the drawing room late. Mr. O, that is, Mr. Osbourne, asked me did I hear all the loud talking this morning about fifteen minutes after eight. I told him that I did hear it. Then Mr. Osbourne asked me did I know who was making such racket early in the morning. I knew but I felt it wouldn't help him, so I decided not to tell him. Once I gave Mr. O that kind of response then he started kidding around with me about being late this morning, and saying that I must have had a late night. I told Mr. O, 'I see someone has gotten up on the right side of the bed and is feeling great.' We both laughed.

"I took his vitals and gave him his meds. Mr. O started to cough, he'd had a cold for a while, and it had both me and his doctor, Dr. Johnston, concerned. The doctor instructed me to watch him closely and see if there were any changes, and to let him know a.s.a.p. That was on Monday morning, it was the last time that I saw Dr. Johnston.

Mr. O began questioning me about some other things, but I can't talk about them just yet. Mr. O started telling me that he was making a lot of changes come tomorrow. He said he planned to make them while he was still alive and breathing in his own body, even if it causes his death! Mr. O said that with such a strong conviction. I could tell Mr. O was getting upset, so I called for Oscar to bring him some tea.

"Then I took his vitals again, and I didn't like the readings that I was getting. I became more concerned about Mr. O, so I tried calling the doctor. Dr. Johnston didn't answer, so I left him a message asking him to come and check Mr. O and to please hurry. I still had Mr. O in view, and I noticed that once he drank some of tea he began to calm down. So, I just let Mr. O rest for a spell as I pondered what he had said to me. Just when I thought it was a good time to ask him some questions about what he had said, Oscar arrived before I could do so.

"Oscar came to take him to lunch in the library, as per Mr. O's request during breakfast. I offered to have lunch with him but he told me 'not this time.' He told me to go and enjoy my lunch since I hadn't had any breakfast. He knew that because I was late this morning. Before leaving for lunch he said he had some papers to go over and something else, which I can't remember at this moment.

"After lunch, I went to the library to see him, to get some much needed answers. When I approached the library door I paused, as I heard laughter coming from on the inside. I stopped and knocked on the door before entering. Upon entering the library I saw that it was Mr. O and Geneva his granddaughter that were laughing. They seemed to be having such a great time together. But as soon as I entered, Geneva left. I thought for a moment 'did she leave because of me?'

"Refocusing, I started over toward Mr. O because it was time for me to take his vitals and give him his meds. I had planned to ask him about the conversation from this morning once he had taken all his afternoon meds. But before I could do or ask anything, Mr. O asked me to get a book for him on the opposite side of the library. By the time I reached the area where the book was, I heard him saying that he couldn't breathe. As I was turning around, I was asking Mr. O what was wrong. I did this while I was rushing over to aid him, but he slumped over. I started CPR as soon as I reached him. In between breaths I was calling out for someone to help. Oscar came and asked what happened. I asked Oscar to call 911, and tell them that Mr.

O was coding. I continued to try to help him until the paramedics arrived and then they took over. It was to no avail-- the paramedic said that Mr. O was gone.

"Round about that same time, Mr. Theodore entered the library with officers in tow, making all kinds of accusations toward me. Blaming and accusing me, of all people, for the murder of his father. Why was Mr. Theodore using the word murder? Why did Mr. Theodore keep saying Mr. O was murdered? Who told him that Mr. O had been murdered? The paramedics had just finished saying that Mr. O was gone, only seconds before Mr. Theodore came into the library. So where and how did Mr. Theodore get that notion in his head so fast that Mr. O was murdered, and Mr. O wasn't even cold yet?" Mr. Straitway assured Odessa that he would get answers to all her questions.

Odessa continued on with her story, telling Mr. Straitway "the officers, they weren't trying to arrest me; they were trying to get answers as to what did happen from the paramedics. That's when the detective came in as they were preparing to remove Mr. O's body from the library. By that time I was very upset, so they got me some water to drink.

"The detective asked the officers to clear the room so he could talk to me. He first said he wanted to get some understanding as to what happened here today in this library. While the detective was yet talking to me I could hear Mr. Theodore in the background accusing me. Mr. Theodore kept stating that he wanted me arrested, which they eventually did. Right after they questioned me, they didn't even hesitate for one moment, they arrested me, and they brought me here. Now, what do I do?"

Mr. Straitway said, "you do nothing. It is my job now to prove your innocence. We have a lot of work ahead of us, so get ready for the trial. I wouldn't be doing you any justice, Odessa, if I didn't warn you that you are about to be hit with everything, yes including the kitchen sink. So brace yourself, and get ready for the ride of your life. It will not stop until this trial is over, one way or the other." Odessa said "I am innocent and God will vindicate me." Mr. Straitway interjected "once again, listen up young lady. God is not on trial here, and they certainly haven't said God has murdered anyone. But you have been arrested for murder. Now Odessa you have to leave all that God stuff out there where it belongs, and not in the courtroom. Mr. Prod will eat you alive and pick his teeth with your bones. Mr. Prod has no use for people who confess to believe in God. Mr. Prod even hates that everyone has to place their hands on the Bible and swear to tell the truth before they can testify. Myself I believe Mr. Prod hates Christians and that may be the very reason he took this case." Odessa spoke out so fast she scared herself, "that 'stuff' as you call it is my life! Outside of Jesus I have no life. He died so that I may live, and I will not leave him out. As a matter of fact I will pray for you that you get to know him. He is my friend and He will get me through everything I have to go through. He is my help. He has always been here for me and always will be. I trust Him with my life, and I pray that He will show you everything you need to know to find the truth. He loves me and I love Him! The truth is out there and God will help you to see it no matter what it takes." Then Mr. Straitway smiled and said "you have a lot of fight in you, and you will need it all of it to stand in this trial. Odessa replied "and with God's help I will stand and I will be victorious."

Once Mr. Straitway felt Odessa was finished talking about her God, he asked her, "so what do you know about the son? There must be some reason that Mr. Theodore targeted you for his father's death. Have the two you ever had words or been at odds before?" Odessa tried very hard to think, and then she replied "not before this morning. I've always tried to stay out of Mr. Theodore's way, whenever he was around. He was always traveling; he's gone most of the time. I'd heard through the household staff grapevine, that he was always attending lots of parties with the bigwigs. They said Mr. Theodore is known for his various kinds of women, and that his motto is 'variety is the spice of life.'

"I don't know how much of this is true. What I do know is true that one lady that Mr. Theodore had dated for a short period of time was very bitter when it was over. I remember her showing up one afternoon last winter uninvited. I'd seen her before prior to that day, when she came to the mansion to see Mr. Theodore. Oscar asked her to wait while he went to get Mr. Teddy for her. As soon Mr. Theodore arrived, she started to shouting at him, 'Teddy you are a lousy two timer and a user, one day you'll get yours!' Mr. Theodore just calmly walked her to the door, and shoveled her out into the cold. Mr. Theodore then started laughing hysterically while he was closing the door.

"Mr. Theodore was still laughing when he saw me coming down the hall. I was headed to my room in the left wing. Then Mr. Theodore called out to me, saying 'Odessa you women are all just alike. Always holding on, when you foreknew it was never going to last from the beginning. You know that we guys just want to sow our oats and then move on to greener pastures.' At that moment, I had no idea as to what Mr. Theodore was even talking about. As I turned to walk up the stairs, Mr. Theodore started laughing even louder, shouting out after me, 'Odessa you know that I'm right.' Later on that day I questioned Oscar as to what Mr. Theodore was referring to when he made that remark and why was it directed at me? That's when I found out what had transpired between Mr. Theodore and the lady visitor.

"Mr. Theodore had never done that before or since. Well, not until this morning. I was not even aware that Mr. Theodore harbored such bad feelings toward me. He hardly ever speaks to me. Even when he enters a room and I'm in there, he always acts as if I'm not there. It's as if I'm invisible to him. He never communicates directly with me. I have always noticed the difference in his treatment toward me since the day that I was hired. It seems as though Mr. Theodore resents me for no apparent reason. Every time I am in his presence, it became very apparent to me and those around that he would purposely slight me. Oscar asked me one day, 'what have you said or done to Mr. Teddy for him to treat you with such disregard? Everyone sees the way Teddy treats you, but not one of us can make heads or tails of it.' I told Oscar that as far as I knew I had done nothing to Mr. Theodore for him to treat me in that manner. My next response to Oscar was 'maybe Mr. Theodore just wanted to be there when I was hired and make the final decision. I was hired by Mr. Harrington Osbourne III. Oscar you yourself know that Mr. Theodore is mainly in charge of hiring new staff or replacing old staff. So I guess since he didn't have any say so in hiring me, maybe that could be or is his reason for solely ignoring me. Whenever it came down to me if Mr. Theodore wanted to tell me or to inform me of any changes, it was always handle indirectly; by way of another staff member.'"

Interrupting her once again, Mr. Straitway asked "so why then on God's green on earth is Mr. Theodore telling the world that you and you alone murdered his father?" "I really haven't got a clue as to when or how all this got started with him" exclaimed Odessa, "but it is clearly all in Mr. Theodore's head. I have never given him any inkling that I was capable of harming anything or anyone, especially not murdering anyone!" Mr. Straitway continued, "Odessa, you really need to understand those are some very strong accusations made by Mr. Theodore, and they will weigh very heavy with any jury. Young lady, you are treading in some deep water, and they're going to try and drown you in it. My job now is to find and get you into a life jacket, and pull you to safety." Odessa was now at a loss for words, she still couldn't believe everything that had taken place. Right after his last comment, Mr. Straitway stood up to leave saying, "if you remember anything else that will be helpful with your defense, just write it down. We will discuss it on my next visit." Odessa nodded okay as Mr. Straitway was leaving.

CHAPTER

7

TEDDY HAD ALWAYS BEEN a brat from his youth. He has had his sights set on running the family business ever since he knew it existed. Teddy spends too much money, and is always investing and freezing assets to show his father that he is worthy to be trusted to run their business. Teddy has had numerous affairs but never married, reasoning that due to the lack of "thoroughbred" (wealthy) women he should wait to meet the right one. Patricia, on the other hand, was top quality and Mr. Osbourne loved her. Like the Osbournes, Patricia was from a very nice, wealthy, and influential family as well-- not like the other women that Teddy would bring around. The women were loud, common, and boisterous. They were not the kind you bring home to meet your parents. Teddy wasn't used to ladies like Patricia, she really was a keeper. He didn't know how to treat her, but he thought that he was putting up a good front. Teddy proposed to Patricia after they had been dating for eight months. Just a little over a year and half into their relationship, Patricia was finally able to see thru all of Teddy's cunning and sly ways. Once she removed her rose colored glasses, she saw Teddy for who he really was and broke it off with him. He was more interested in Patricia's family's business than in her. Teddy would try to get tips from Patricia about the business or other things that she and her father had talked about. Teddy would use that information for investing strategies and bragging rights. Patricia's father hired a private investigator to get the scoop on Teddy, but before the P.I. had gathered all his information, Patricia dropped Teddy for good. Teddy never thought Patricia was as smart as she was, so he tried to take advantage of her by trying to extract valuable information from her. When their brief engagement was called off, Teddy vowed to never get that close to another woman. Especially when any talk about marriage would get started, Teddy would steer himself as far away as possible. His purpose for proposing to Patricia was really only to get in good with his father. Teddy has only ever loved one person, true and blue without any reservations, and the person that he is head over heels in love with is Teddy himself. Now as for Teddy's love for money and power they take precedence over everything in his life.

It was late when the guards returned to Odessa's cell. Looking around, she noticed that the guard had left a dinner tray for her. She was thankful for the food, but she really didn't have an appetite. Odessa was so caught up in all that happened that whole miserable day-- being blamed for murdering her friend, and then being told she has to be proven innocent. "I am innocent! What happened? Why does Mr. Theodore feel that I could do such a thing?" Drained from all the thoughts running thru her mind, she went over and sat down on her bed. She began to break down and cry, feeling sorry for her-self. It was at that very moment she said "Odessa, get a hold of your-self." Feeling herself beginning to relax, she knew that it was time to do something. Collecting her thoughts, she knew there was only one thing to do; it was in time to pray. She started off by praying for herself, but suddenly her prayers began to shift in another direction. She prayed, "Lord please help Mr. Straitway as well as all the other people handling my defense." She continued on praying even harder for those who were persecuting her. Once she had finished, she felt a sense of peace and curled up to get some much needed rest, whis-pering yet another prayer for her family, loved ones, and her church before falling to sleep.

Back at the mansion Geneva has gone to bed and is having what she feels is a haunting nightmare. She continues to see shadows of the day of the accident. In this dream, she and her parents are always in their family car and her dad is driving. Her dad always turns and looks over at her mother, who is sitting on the front passenger side. He's telling her that something is wrong, and all she can make out of their conversation is *Teddy*. The next memory has always been, just as in times past, Geneva would awaken in the hospital with her grandfather sitting in the chair next to her bed-- but not this time. Geneva would wake from this recurring dream afraid, scared, a bit confused, and always in a cold sweat. Lately, Geneva has been having this dream more than ever. Never really knowing what or why, she has been haunted by it for years because she really wants to hear and understand what her parents are talking about. When Geneva was younger and she'd have those same bad nightmares, and she could always run and jump into her grandfather's bed. He would always console her, giving her warm milk and cookies, then he'd hold her until she fell asleep. Geneva began to cry, asking herself how she was able to do such a terrible thing to someone that loved her so dearly. That night Geneva cried herself to sleep feeling all alone, wishing she could talk to her grandfather just one more time, yet remembering her Uncle Teddy's words that her Grandfather didn't love her the same way, Geneva fell asleep angry at Odessa.

At a small out of the way diner, Teddy and Mr. Johns are having yet another secret meeting about the events of the day. Teddy told Mr. Johns how it took a lot of convincing on his part to get them to arrest Odessa. Once they finally listened and came to their senses, they arrested Odessa. Mr. Johns asked Teddy what Odessa's reaction was when they arrested her. Teddy began to laugh, saying "Odessa was in such a shock when I walked in the library with the officers accusing her of murdering my father. She looked as if a ton of bricks had just caved in on her. She's probably still trying to declare her innocence, with not a leg to stand on. I saw her rubbing that glue on her hand, and I pointed it out to one of the officers. He then made the detective in charge aware of it, and they took a sample of it right there. I set Odessa up and I hung her, just as we planned. All of the staff will side with me, and collaborate my story, especially if they all want to remain gainfully employed. I have trained them all in the lying department, but that Oscar is the only one that worries me."

Mr. Johns started screaming at Teddy, "fool why are you laughing? From where I am sitting you still have a few loose ends to tie up. Did you find out the combination number? Did you find and talk to that mechanic? Teddy he's not going to just show up anywhere is he?" Teddy said he is where no one will be able to find him. "Right. Teddy-- what if he's found, will he talk? I told you that your father said he had new information about the accident, and that he'd plan to bring charges against everyone that was involved. If you haven't covered all your tracks, you better make darn sure you do it immediately, and before the trial." Mr. Teddy wasn't laughing now; he knew he'd better take care of it, and right away. Remembering from some past experiences, Teddy knew that Mr. Johns would not be a good adversary. He also knew he'd better never take Mr. Johns lightly.

Mr. Johns was not a person you wanted to mess with; he had ties and connections everywhere. He could get people to do just about anything: he's already gotten Teddy to kill off all of his family, except for Geneva. He doesn't care who he steps on, he just cares about money and power. Mr. Johns and his associates make Teddy and others like him get their hands dirty, but never himself: he stays clear of all of that. He's the one that would inform Teddy about any changes in his father's will-- for a fee, of course. Mr. Johns started off receiving large amounts of cash from Teddy, but then he saw the bigger picture of the business, so he started to exchange the information in lieu of stock in the family business once Mr. Harrington Osbourne III died. He put it in writing and had Teddy sign it. Then Mr. Johns and his associates would own a large percentage of *their* company when Teddy took over. This would be for legal services rendered, or so he says. Mr. Johns has been feeding Teddy information for years, but in the last few months he's really been pushing it Teddy's way. Mr. Johns has been so busy with Teddy, he has been slipping and is not aware of it. Mr. Johns has been falsifying so many documents, and creating other ones, that he's not cleaning up after himself as well as he should. There's all kinds of incriminating evidence floating around Mr. Johns' office in plain sight, so it wouldn't take much for the *wrong* person to see it and connect him to the *right* people.

CHAPTER

Odessa is still locked up, as the judge denied her bail at the hearing. Mr. Straitway has been coming by her cell, keeping her informed on what is happening with her case. He said the prosecutors are pushing for a speedy trial, and Mr. Prod is trying to get Judge Watts to move it up on his docket. Odessa looked kind of weary after Mr. Straitway said that, but he reassured her not to worry; things have a way of working themselves out.

Besides feeling scared and lonely, Odessa hasn't really had an appetite. Wanting terribly to see her dad, some family, or friends, Odessa can't help feeling like she's being isolated. Since her arrest, she has not been in touch with the real world. She has been locked up for a couple of weeks now, and somehow they seem to have thrown the keys away. Had they forgotten that she was there? Did they plan to keep her there forever? Other prisoners were receiving visits, why wasn't she, why had they denied Odessa that privilege? That was a question for Mr. Straitway the next time he visited her. Even though Odessa wasn't a murderer, she was still locked up and being treated as such. This has caused her a lot of sleepless and restless nights. Now she is really starting to be concerned about her whole situation. She never gets to see anyone except for Mr. Straitway whenever he comes to visit her. Other than that, the only other people Odessa can look forward to seeing are the prison staff coming around at mealtime with trays, either dropping off or picking them up.

It was very early in the morning when Odessa awakens from her so called nap. As Odessa opened her eyes, she sees that it is still twilight, the stars are still out. Odessa blessed and thanked God for a new day. Expressing to Him her love for Him and telling Him how thankful she is for all that He has done for her. "Lord, I don't understand, but you know all, please intervene on my behalf. Father, please don't allow the enemy to triumph over me. You have all power, so please use it to help me in this situation. I thank you and I bless you amen." Still feeling tired she laid down on her bed, falling back to sleep.

A few hours have passed; Odessa is startled awake by the sound of the guard's voice telling everyone it was time for breakfast. Odessa got up and prepared herself for the day very fast, with barely enough time to catch her tray as the guard shoved it into her little cell window. These little windows were cut into the bars of each cell. She was told it was how everyone received clean towels and linen, food, or any mail, or any outside communication. One thing that was scary-- it was thru this same window that they would handcuff you.

After lunch, Odessa was told that there was a visitor waiting for her. When she entered the room, her best friend Lisa was sitting down at a table. Odessa went over to her; they hugged for a few moments then sat down to talk. Lisa told Odessa that the police came to their apartment with a search warrant. "It was mainly for your bedroom and the common areas of the apartment. And they did just that." She told Odessa that they did find some things, and they placed them into clear bags and took them when they finally left. "They didn't let me see what they were taking. I was asked to stay in my room and out of their way while they did their job. And they told me when it was okay for me to come out, mainly when they were finished. I overheard them say something about Mr. Osbourne had been poisoned. They really made a mess, I'm still cleaning up the place, but it's okay. Odessa, what happened?" Odessa told her what happened and because "Mr. Theodore accused me of his father's death, they arrested me." Lisa said she was sorry, and then asked Odessa what she could do, if anything at all, to help her. Odessa paused and began to think, and then she asked "did they search your room at all?" She said "no, why?" Odessa said she had hidden something in there that Mr. O had given her. "It's under the carpet in your closet, all the way in the back. It's a plastic bag with a couple of envelopes, that's the one of the last things Mr. O asked me about the day he died. He said it had instructions in it to call someone for help." Odessa asked her to get it but not to open the envelope, but to follow the instructions on the outside of the envelope that is addressed to her only-- *Odessa*. Then Lisa was to put the other things back in the plastic where she had found them.

Then she gave Lisa some specific instructions to follow. Odessa asked Lisa not to tell anyone about their conversation until she tells her to do so. Then Lisa began catching Odessa up on a few other things that have been happening. When their visit was over, they hugged again and said goodbye. Odessa knew she could trust Lisa with her life.

A few weeks passed after Lisa's visit, and Odessa began to wonder if she was okay, and if all was going well with her. Odessa could hardly wait for their next visit, to find out what is was that Mr. O had given her.

Between juggling her job and other parts of her life, Lisa has been very busy since her visit with Odessa. She has been following all her instructions to the letter, including the instructions on the envelope. Lisa knew Odessa was depending on her, and she wasn't about to let her down. She has been trying to reach the man on the envelope as instructed; and she has left him a few messages. Now Lisa feels the only thing to do is just wait until he contacts her. She believes he may be the only person that could give her some insight on how to help her friend. Odessa knows that they have set the trial to start in a few weeks. Now there are only two options for her: sit on her hands and wait; or began to pray, going into spiritual warfare. Odessa chose the latter of the two.

CHAPTER

9

ODESSA ENTERED THE COURTROOM escorted by two guards on the first day of the trial. She looked around the room, while taking in all that was going on. She was warned that this was going to be a very big political case. She was on trial for the murder of a very wealthy and influential businessman, and everyone wanted to watch it with front row seats. They were acting exactly like Mr. Straitway had said they would: as if they all were at a circus or something, just without the hot dogs, popcorn, peanuts, and please don't forget the cotton candy. The courtroom was filling up so fast with all kinds of people that were there for all sorts of different reasons. This was all new to Odessa, and kind of scary too. There was the media, witnesses, spectators, some of Odessa's family and church members, and of course don't forget the naysayers. There was even some talk going behind her among a few of them, as if they had all gathered for a lynching. Taking her seat, she continued to look around the room. Still trying to see into the crowd, she finally spotted her dad standing there in the midst of all of those people. He was smiling right at her; his smile made her feel somewhat at ease.

Then Odessa noticed the prosecutor's witnesses all sat near the back on the same side as the prosecutor's table. That is where she spotted Mr. Theodore, but she couldn't seem to see Geneva. Then Odessa looked directly across at the prosecutor's table. The prosecutors were all dressed in dark suits, and were seated at their table on the right side of the room. All around them were all kinds of files, and boxes everywhere. Prosecutor Prod began talking loudly and looking across at the defense table, telling his team "we'd better put some of this stuff out of sight before the defense tries to come out swinging, even though we know they don't even have a weapon to swing with!" All of Mr. Prod's team started to chuckle.

At the defense table, Mr. Straitway looked at Doris and said "there they go with all their shenanigans." Doris looked away, and started to look through some notes and files on the case before court began. Mr. Straitway, speaking to Odessa: "how are you holding up?" Her response was, "as well as could be expected, seeing I'm on trial for murder." Mr. Straitway told Odessa to "never let them see you sweat. You just keep looking straight ahead all through this trial. Their whole strategy is based on trying to scare you to death. You say you're innocent, and we are going to prove it."

Then he whispered, "Hi Lord it's me, Barry Straitway. I know that I don't talk to you much. Lord I need your help; I don't feel I can win this case without you. I'm not asking you for myself, I'm asking you to intervene on Odessa's behalf in this trail to prove her innocence. If you don't want to help me, do it for Odessa. You are all she talks about, Odessa really believes in you."

No sooner than Mr. Straitway finished his short prayer, the bailiff asked everyone to rise as the Honorable Judge Watts was entering the courtroom. Judge Watts has been having a weird dream every night since he placed this trial on his docket. In the dream, he steps up to the bench to sit down in his chair, but instead he starts to fall. When Judge Watts starts falling, it is into an utter darkness: everything is all black and he can't see his hands in front of his face. He tries very hard to find something to grasp and hold on to, but he can't. He just keeps falling and is unable to stop himself because there seems to be no bottom. He can hear some weird noises, but when he calls out for help, no one ever answers. What if that is what hell is really like; is there really any proof that hell exists? No fault on Judge Watts' part for not knowing the answer-- he was raised by people who didn't believe in God, and didn't mind letting everyone around them know it. Somehow, even though Judge Watts was taught that way, he's always wanted to know if Jesus Christ really exists and is there a heaven.

Judge Watts said "the case before us today is the State of Illinois versus the defendant, Odessa Princeton. Prosecutor Prod for the state, and Attorney Straitway for the defense." Mr. Prod is one who has sold his soul for money, fame, and power. He is what one would call a devil worshipper. Mr. Prod hates anyone and everyone who is remotely believed to be a Christian. Mr. Prod will go after them relentlessly, with everything he's got and can or conjure up. Depending on what your stand in life is, you will either love Mr. Prod or wish him dead before your trial.

Judge Watts asked the bailiff to let the jurors into the court, saying "they are all here and ready to proceed with this trail, right?" The bailiff opened the door for the jurors to enter the courtroom. As the jurors began to take their seats, the judge noticed that juror #9 was missing. He ordered the bailiff to go find Juror # 9 and bring him back, but the bailiff came back empty-handed. He informed the judge that juror #9 had gotten really sick and was taken to the hospital to be checked out.

Instantly the judge asked the attorneys to approach the bench. He informed them juror # 9 had been removed and they were to interview more jurors to pick an alternate to replace him by the end of the business day. Then Judge Watts asked Mr. Prod and Mr. Straitway if they had any questions? They both said "no" at the same time, as if they were harmonizing. The judge said "okay", then asked them to return to their seats.

Judge Watts, speaking to the entire court, stated "due to a missing juror, the court has decided to close for today while the attorneys attend to their task of selecting another juror. I am confident that they will fulfill their duties to the satisfaction of this court by the end of this business day. This court will reconvene at ten o'clock sharp on tomorrow morning so that this trial can get on its way, without fail." After his ruling the judge exited the courtroom.

Once the judge left, Odessa asked Mr. Straitway what was happening? What did all this mean for her? The guard began to cuff

Odessa to take her back to her cell. Mr. Straitway asked Odessa not to worry and said he would see her later. As they were leading Odessa out of the courtroom, she took a final sweep of the courtroom with her eyes. She saw her dad again; he was still smiling at her as he had done earlier. Odessa also observed Mr. Theodore leaving the courtroom and pushing Geneva out ahead of himself. Geneva was looking back as well in Odessa's direction, with a strange look on her face.

In the car on the way back to the mansion, and still troubled by her dreams, Geneva decided to talk to her uncle about her disturbing dreams. She told him she could see that her parents were upset and heard them say his name. "The next thing that I remember was waking up in the hospital. What is this all about Uncle Teddy? Can you tell me why did they look so scared and were saying your name?" Teddy got quiet for a moment; he didn't want to jump the gun and say the wrong thing. He surely didn't want Geneva to become suspicious of him, and knew this was the time he had to tread lightly. He started off by first trying to console her, telling her it was alright, it was only a dream. "You have suffered a deep loss, and that would be enough to cause you to start thinking about your parents." Geneva said "but that doesn't explain the looks on their faces when they said your name, Uncle Teddy." Not being able to hold his peace any farther, Teddy blurted out "your father didn't like me, he was jealous of my relationship with you! Freddrick always felt you loved me more than him. He said it on several occasions, and Rebecca knew it too. We all tried to make Freddrick feel comfortable and to reassure him, but every time he saw you hugging me, he would get a sort of strange look on his face. That's probably the look you saw that day." Then Teddy hugged Geneva really tight, (one would say too tight) "you know I have always loved you. Haven't I always been like a second father to you, right?" Geneva nodded in agreement, but something just didn't feel right. Deep down on the inside Geneva was screaming "what really happened to my parents?", but she dare not ask her Uncle Teddy another question.

When they arrived back at the mansion, Geneva went straight to her room. She didn't understand the accusations that her uncle had made about her father. Uncle Teddy had made her feel so uncomfortable. Geneva had never ever heard him mention that her father was jealous of Uncle Teddy. Where is all this coming from? Somehow that still doesn't explain away her mother's facial expression. At that moment, Geneva decided not to say anything else about her dreams to her uncle. Uncle Teddy seemed kind of edgy and agitated when he was talking about her parents. Now Geneva really wanted to find out what they were talking about that last time she remembered seeing them alive.

Back in her cell Odessa couldn't make heads or tails of what had happened in court. She started to pray, "Lord what's really going on? Father you know all things and you said that all things work together for our good. Please help me to endure whatever is ahead of me and help Mr. Theodore's mind and heart." Before the untimely death of Mr. O, she would pray what we call light prayers. Nowadays, her prayers are more serious, and more directed. Deep down in her heart the words from the Holy Bible have begun to speak to her situation. Remembering the words from Matthew 5:44, "But I say unto you Love your enemies, bless them that curse you, do good to them that hate you, and pray for them which despitefully use you, and persecute you." She has been praying with all her heart for everyone who attached to her case in any way, shape, form or fashion.

As other thoughts began to invade her mind, she started wondering where Ned could have gone. "Hasn't he read the newspapers about Mr. O's death, why hasn't he come to see me?" During Odessa's eye search, she didn't see Ned in court today. Mr. Straitway told her he hadn't been able to locate Ned, and he would be a good character witness, if they could only find him in time. Mr. Straitway's sources informed him that Ned had moved, left no forwarding address, and had closed all his bank accounts. It seemed Ned had covered his tracks so well that he didn't want to be found.

Odessa couldn't believe he just disappeared for good, without even a goodbye. As she traveled back in time thru her mind, she began to reminisce about the first day that she met Ned. He had just showed up at her church one Sunday morning service. After service he came right over to speak to her, out of all the young single ladies that were there that day. He said hi, and asked if she would please forgive his forwardness in saying "you are so beautiful that you just glow. May, I please share in some of your light, how about I take you to dinner?" Odessa began to blush; no one had ever said that about her. Once she stopped blushing some, he introduced himself. "I'm Ned Tamper, and what might your name be?" Smiling widely Odessa answered him, "my name is Odessa." Then he said "your name sends chills up and down my spine, it has such a beautiful ring to it. I know every time your name is mentioned all of the angels began to sing." Before he could go on any farther with his compliments, her dad and some family members came over to see who she was talking to. Right away her dad started questioning her. "So Odessa, who is this young fellow that is going to make us all late for Sunday dinner?" Odessa couldn't stop smiling, so Ned introduced himself. Then her dad did something he had never done before: he invited a total stranger to dinner. Not just any dinner-- it was for their family and it was known as "only family members' dinner". From that day on, her and Ned began having standard Sunday dates after dinner. For special occasions, she and Ned would go out on Saturday's.

Odessa loved her job but she looked forward to seeing her family and Ned on the weekend. Ned had made it a tradition that after each date, the next day he would send Odessa flowers or candy --sometimes both-- with a card stating how great of a time he'd had, and how he was so looking forward to their next date. They had been dating for a while when he started discussing their futures. Ned asked her if she ever would marry and have children. She said it all depends on who is asking. They both laughed, and that subject never came up again. But, Odessa felt they were drawing closer to that place in their lives. She really believed that Ned was falling in love with her. Without a doubt she knew had definitely been smitten by him. Lately he had been asking her a lot more about work. They had discussed their jobs previously, but now it seemed he wanted to know a lot about her talks with Mr. O. These talks made her feel a little uncomfortable, but she really didn't see any harm in answering his questions. He only asked those types of question when they were alone at one of those out of the way restaurants. But he never started the conversations off like that; he would just manage to bring their conversation around to it. She didn't really have much to say about her duties other than she liked her job and she and Mr. O are friends. Ned never really talked about his past, but they had talked about hers briefly.

CHAPTER
10

Now RESIDING IN CALIFORNIA, Ned heard about the trial. Mr. Johns called him before it even got started, and when he spoke to Ned, his voice had a very serious and threatening tone to it. Mr. Johns told Ned not to even think about coming back to Illinois to try and help Odessa. Mr. Johns and his associates had Ned make incriminating statements about Odessa. Mr. Johns further warned Ned about getting his emotions involved in their plan, and that it was not what he was being paid for. He reminded Ned at the same time, "we know everything there is to know about you-- everything!" Ned had never heard Mr. Johns raise his voice before, that time but he knew he better not cross Mr. Johns. Ned really did care for Odessa, but he was only there as their plant. Ned wondered how it might have been if he and Odessa had met under other circumstances. Ned truly wished that there was a way that he could contact Odessa without Mr. Johns and his associates finding out, but he felt he shouldn't rock any boats, for fear of himself becoming a disposable pawn in their scheme. There are so many things Ned had wanted to say to Odessa, but the right time never presented itself. Mr. Johns always had someone watching and listening in on their private conversations. The associates recorded Ned and Odessa any time they were on the phone, so that they would always have leverage over him. Ned's precise orders from Mr. Johns were to always follow the script that one of the associates would leave for him at each of the different restaurants. But no one, not even Ned himself, counted on him developing real and true feelings for Odessa. That's the reason why Ned would send the flowers and candy without anyone ever knowing about it. That wasn't part of their plan-- that was all Ned. Sometimes at night, he wanted to call Odessa back after the taped call, but he didn't know if they were still listening in somehow. Often upon returning to his apartment after their date, Ned always felt a strange sort of feeling, as if someone had been there in his apartment. That same paranoia would cause Ned to check his place for over an hour, before he could settle down and retire for the evening. Ned was really glad that part of his life was behind him now, or so he hoped. Ned didn't really know what he had gotten himself into when he agreed to their terms when they first approached him. Ned just thought he'd make some easy money, and then would get a better paying job in another state and so he could live it up. What difference would it make? Ned didn't know Odessa, she was just a job--or was she? Most of the time, Ned would convince himself that someone else was going to make the money, so why not him? What Ned didn't realize was that once you got something from the associates' purse, there were real strings attached to it.

It's really getting late, yet Teddy is still in his office at the mansion, burning the midnight oil. Teddy has been trying hard for weeks to tie up all his loose ends. He's afraid if he doesn't cover his tracks, some of Mr. Johns' associates will happily oblige him, even if he is on the tracks. He's been trying hard to reach Chester Browning, without any success. Chester was one of the estate's mechanics; they paid him to fix the brakes on Freddy's car to make it look like an accident. Once he was done, they paid him twenty thousand dollars to leave town, never to show his face again. Teddy and Mr. Johns both did their research before hiring Chester to kill Rebecca and her husband. Once they knew Chester had a gambling problem, he instantly became the right man for job. Chester was known to run off at the mouth a lot, and that's why Mr. Johns wanted Teddy to do some reinforcement. Mr. Johns knew if Chester ever started talking around the wrong people there could be problems for everyone, including him. But before Mr. Johns would go down, Chester would be buried so far and so deep no one would ever find him.

The reason that Mr. Teddy and his sources can't find Chester is because he's in jail in Ohio, awaiting trial for attempted murder. Chester tried fixing his sister's in law brakes-- he felt that he had gotten away with it once before, why not try it again? He knew his wife had an insurance policy on her sister, and he needed money to pay off his debts. So when his sister-in-law died, they could collect the insurance money. Chester's wife had no clue what he was up to, and once she found out, she agreed to testify against him. He is in a lot of trouble now and he knows it.

When things looked like they were never going to go Chester's way again, he received a visit from a total stranger who offered to help him out of his situation. Chester had been down about being locked up, but he began to feel that the cards were once again stacked in his favor and he is thanking his lucky stars for shining down on him once again. Why did Chester get so excited? Right after Chester was contacted by this stranger about Rebecca's accident, he just felt he had a way out, a second chance. Everyone, including Chester, knew that he wasn't going to pass up a chance to get out of jail and start his life over somewhere else, even though he is now all by himself because his wife wants nothing more to do with him. But he doesn't care, and really he can't afford to. He told the stranger that he would only spill his guts about what happened the day Rebecca died and who had hired him if and only if they got Chester exactly what he was asking for. His demands were a top notch defense attorney, fifty thousand dollars, and of course no charges against him once he helped them. He said he would help them, but Chester was really helping himself. Chester was always working on the next con, and if people didn't know him, they trusted him. He sought out victims and preyed on their weaknesses, just like Mr. Teddy and his bunch sought him.

CHAPTER
11

BACK AT THE MANSION, everyone is restless. Mr. Teddy can't sleep because all his leads on Chester are coming up as dead ends. And Teddy can't tell Mr. Johns and his associates that he hasn't found Chester. He has been dodging their phone calls, hoping that he can just stumble upon any information concerning Chester's whereabouts before he has to talk to Mr. Johns. Teddy is planning on making some calls in the morning but he is very worried about how Mr. Johns will react to his news, or rather the lack of news. With that, he turns over and tries to get some much needed sleep, seeing that it's now 2 a.m. and he knows he doesn't have much time to rest.

Odessa isn't the only one that hasn't rested since Mr. O's untimely death. Geneva is still having her haunting nightmares more frequently. Now she is even having them in the daytime, and she has not been able to sleep in weeks since her grandfather died. She might as well be in prison with Odessa, because she is already in a prison of her own choosing: it's in her soul. Geneva can't get away from herself; it's her own conscience that is condemning her. Geneva is being pulled in so many directions each day, especially by those deep dreadful thoughts, with no way out. What happened to Geneva to cause her to choose hate over love? How could Geneva help anyone kill her loving grandfather? All Geneva did was place a patch on her grandfather's chest, and she couldn't even finish the job, because that lying, cheating thief Odessa came in. "Grandfather had clearly chosen Odessa over me, it's entirely his fault! Grandfather was the one that kept changing his will so much that I couldn't keep up. Why was grandfather so against me, I loved him so, but he loved Odessa? I guess it was partly Odessa's fault too, but just how did Odessa get grandfather to turn against me, his only grandchild? Odessa deserves to be in jail even if she didn't do it. She has hurt me so bad, now it is time for her to pay for all the pain that she has caused me and my family. But even with Odessa in jail, my pain just isn't satisfied nor is it going away. Why don't I feel good about setting Odessa up? Why, did Uncle Teddy choose Odessa?" But was Geneva truly sure about everything, and if so, then why can't she rest?

Geneva has been trying to embrace her dreams lately, and not block anything out. She feels if she can face her fears, then maybe she'd be able to figure out what happened to her parents. She really wants to know if her Uncle Teddy was involved. "Maybe that's why Uncle Teddy didn't want me to talk to grandfather about our secret conversations. I always wanted to ask grandfather about the changes in the wills that I saw just lying around, but why were the wills outside of the safe? Grandfather was always careful when it came to dealing with business matters. Was all of it just one big scheme? Why did I have to help with the great send off, sending grandfather off to an early grave? Uncle Teddy always was always telling me that grandfather was terminally ill and it was affecting his whole body, especially grandfather's mind. How did Uncle Teddy know this, and how come grandfather never told me that he was terminally ill? Why such a vicious plan to kill grandfather, and what was the rush if he was already going to die? That day will always be the second saddest day of my life." Geneva, not being able to think anymore, said "Uncle Teddy used me to help kill the grandfather I loved so dearly. What was I supposed to gain from grandfather's death? How did he convince me to do it? Was it all because someone kept leaving me all those poisonous bread crumbs everywhere?"

Geneva didn't know she was just a pawn in her Uncle Teddy's scheme to kill his own father. Teddy had cooked up this deadly plan years ago, long before he started playing mind games with Geneva. From the first day Odessa came to work, Teddy planned to set her up for his father's murder. Odessa would be Teddy's scapegoat. She was the lamb that Teddy had planned to sacrifice and slaughter from the very beginning. No one but his father knew how evil Teddy could be. From the time he was a little child, Mr. O could see that Teddy's love of money would eventually be his downfall. But did Mr. O really know what Teddy was really capable of doing for it? He tried keeping a watchful eye on Teddy and keeping him on a short leash, but Teddy was even more cunning than Mr. O expected. That's why he tried to keep Odessa out of Teddy's range of fire. Mr. O never thought that in a million years that Teddy would be capable of killing and planning anyone's murder.

In the beginning Geneva got along very well with Odessa, until her uncle started filling her head with all sorts of lies pertaining to Odessa. Next, Teddy started to put his plan into motion, placing the next piece in his puzzle. The plan was to poison Geneva's mind against both of them; his father, and Odessa. He was always filling her head with all sorts of bad thoughts, and periodically telling her "Odessa is going to take your mother's place. Father is planning on adopting her, isn't he always saying that she reminds him of Rebecca? You've heard father say it yourself, haven't you? Didn't father use to spend all his free time with you Geneva, but now look at him; he's spending all of it with Odessa." Teddy made Geneva believe those lies and all of the other ones he made sure he showed Geneva indirectly. He did it all by carefully placing false documents around secured areas of the mansion, where he was assured that Geneva would surely find and read them. He made sure that he highlighted Geneva's name and the changes to the amounts of what she would be receiving, knowing good and well she would read it. Each time she saw the will, Geneva was getting less and less, and Odessa was getting more and more. Teddy always added his touches, and his clinchers were the phrases *to my loving daughter Odessa and to my granddaughter Geneva*, to make Geneva think her grandfather loved Odessa and not her. He would always say, "father is losing his edge when it comes to Odessa." When they were looking at the fake documents, and he made sure to tell her that her grandfather was going to end up leaving her destitute and penniless. He'd announce to Geneva that their lifestyles would change drastically, all because "father is going to leave everything to Odessa, her church, and their charities. Father, doesn't care anymore about what will happen to us once he's gone. I heard father say to someone on the phone that 'they better enjoy this type of living while I'm still alive, because when I'm gone they are done.'" Teddy of course was lying to her, but Geneva didn't know the truth. She just blindly trusted and took him at his word. With those haunting words tormenting Geneva each day, she had to make a decision of what path to take. When Geneva made her final choice, she had many regrets and did not want to harm the grandfather that she loved. She really didn't want to put the patch on her grandfather; he truly was a good hearted and loving person, but her uncle forced her to do it. Geneva's Uncle Teddy has a great influence over her, one she can't tear herself away from; she was trapped in his deadly clutches. Teddy forcefully explained it to Geneva this way: "when father is gone it will be only the two of us, and we have to look out for one another."

Theodore Osbourne, knows that the things that he has been filling Geneva head with are lies; so very far from the truth. Teddy knows his father would never do what he has been describing to Geneva, because she is the one greatest joy and the highlight of Mr. O's life. Ever since Geneva could walk and talk and she said the word grandpa, you could always find her at her grandfather's desk in the library. She would be hanging around, kissing his neck, and telling her grandfather how much she loves him. You could find them joking and laughing anytime. Mr. O has always provided for Geneva, and told her that he had planned to do so even when he is gone.

CHAPTER
12

THE TRIAL HAS STARTED up again and it's time for the opening
remarks. Judge Watts tells the prosecution that they are up first and
then the defense in that order.

Mr. Prod starts out by telling the jurors, and all that are in
the sound of his voice, that the prosecution will show not only that
the defendant is guilty of murdering the deceased, but that she had
motive and the opportunity as well to commit this murder. "Odessa
Princeton was cut out of the deceased's will, and she was angry, yes
angry enough to murder! We will prove to you beyond a shadow
of doubt that the defendant, Odessa Princeton, is a murderer and
a liar trying to hide behind the church and her Christian beliefs.
The defense would have you to believe that Christians don't kill, but
given the right circumstances they will and she," pointing to Odessa
"the defendant, did murder her employer. He was helpless and at her
mercy. She was his nurse. Wasn't Odessa supposed to help him get
well? That's all the prosecution has to say until you hear from our
eye-witnesses." Then he went back to his seat with a very smug look
on his face.

Mr. Straitway opened by saying, "the prosecution has planned
on making this case not to be about just the murder, but about my
client's beliefs. We all believe in something or other, but that doesn't
mean because you or you (Pointing at the jurors) may have more
than me, and then I should kill you for it. No, absolutely not, as the

prosecution said you just get angry and go out and commit a murder. The defense will prove to you that the defendant, Odessa Princeton is innocent! And that someone other than the defendant had an even bigger motive and better opportunity to murder the deceased."

Once both sides finished their opening remarks, it was time for the prosecution to call their various witnesses to the stand. You can surely bet that Mr. Prod has been examining numerous of witnesses. Some of them were people who use to attend Odessa's church. He even was able to find the one young lady who Odessa had beat in a teen pageant back in high school. Mr. Prod had yet another witness who said that she was dating Ned first, and Odessa stole him away from her. But that wasn't all: the witness said Odessa had threatened her life, and if she didn't stay away from Ned, Odessa will for sure do her some bodily harm. Then there was the police report filed by that same woman, but it was later proven that she had been treated for psychiatric disorders and was currently under a doctor's care. During Mr. Straitway's cross examination it was proven that it was really the other way around-- that Odessa was the victim and not the other woman.

Mr. Prod just kept calling them one right after another. He didn't just question them about the murder, but about Odessa's religious beliefs. Mr. Prod paraded the witnesses through the courtroom like the court was really a circus, and he's the ringmaster. Knowing fully well that all those types of stunts usually just tend to confuse the jurors, and that is exactly how Mr. Prod wanted them to be: so confused they didn't even have a clue what the case was really about. Mr. Prod was showing and telling the jurors only what he wanted them to believe, and above all what he wanted them to remember once they began their deliberations. Trying his best to destroy and diminish Odessa's character, Mr. Prod loved to assassinate every person that confessed to be a Christian. Once Mr. Prod felt he has accomplished that, then he goes straight for the jugular, spilling as much blood as he possibly could without killing his victims. He wanted just enough blood for the jurors to see and become thirsty for more; rendering a guilty verdict so that their thirst will be satisfied.

That evening Odessa's dad came to visit her, and she was so excited to see him. Once the guard removed her handcuffs, she ran right into her father's opened arms. He hugged and held her close for some time. Odessa began to cry, and then dad held her even tighter, at the same time consoling her and saying" everything is alright, I'm here." Still crying she asked him "why haven't you come to visit me before now, and why is all of this happening to me? Why did Mr. Teddy accuse me of his father's murder, out of all the people in that big house? What have I ever done to him, that he hates me so much?" Her dad explained that he had taken sick, and he made everyone promise not to utter one word about it. "So that's why no one has been here. Odessa, we all knew that you would have asked all kinds of questions, so they just stayed away. Now that I'm better you will receive visits from everyone." "I thought you all had left me and wrote me off. I didn't know what to think, when I didn't see you, after that first day of the trial. Oh Daddy, I have missed you so, I felt so alone." Sitting down, he said "Odessa, you know that I love you, don't you? You know that I would have never left you without a good reason. But Odessa, you must always remember that God is the one that said He would never leave you nor forsake you. Where is God in all this, has He left you? Most definitely not, He is the one who said He will stick closer than a brother. He is the one that provides for you." He hugged her again, trying to calm her down. "I trust Him with my life as well as yours.

"Odessa, you remember saying you wanted to be used by Him? Well we never know how He will do it when we ask. Nor do we have a clue of how, when, or where He will do it. And furthermore, we can't tell Him how to do His job. He created everything--including all of us-- it's all up to Him, and it's in His timing. Now you are in your finest hour and it's your chance to shine for the Lord. Maybe you are supposed to be a light in this dark place for those who have don't know the true Light. To help light up the pathways for the many lost souls out there. Odessa you must stand up straight and tall for your God, the One that you talk about continuously. Doesn't it say in Matthew 5: 16 let your light so shine before men, that they may see your good works, and glorify your Father which is in Heaven. You must always remember if God is for you he is more than the world against you. If you must be the example, so be it, and stand tall and shine as bright as the stars on a dark night and as bright as the sun on a bright summer day during this trial.

"You are the only Christ that some of these people in here will ever see. Odessa, what does the Word say about your situation? And you know what I'm talking about, the part that's about all the chosen people." "Daddy, that's in Matthew 20:16. It says; So the last shall be first, and the first last: for many are called but few chosen." "Aren't you the one always asking God to use you? You wanted to be used by Him didn't you? When we ask God to use us, we truly never know if or how He's going to do it. But as soon as we get into an uncomfortable place we start asking, where is He? He's right here, just like He was with the three Hebrews in the fiery furnace. Just like He was right there with Daniel in the Lion's den, locking the mouths of the lions. Just like He was when we lost your mother and my wife. He is still here, can't you feel Him? One day I will leave this Earth, but God will always be here. We don't choose our assignments, God chooses them for us. Because He knows just what we need and how much we need. He knows how long or how short each trial should be. Odessa, you have to trust Him with you very life. In Matthew 10:39 Jesus clearly says He that findeth his life shall lose it: and he that loseth his life for my sake shall find it."

"Daddy how can they keep saying that I killed Mr. O? He was my friend." "I don't know the answer to that, but God knows it. We have to trust that the truth will prevail. One thing that I know deep down in my heart is that God is at the helm of this ship. You will be free to raise your sails again. You will soar as the eagle once again. Odessa this is only a test of your faith, embrace it and pass it. One day you will look back on this time and you will rejoice because God gave you the victory over your enemies." Odessa chuckled a little. Her dad asked "is that a smile I see?" Then Odessa smiled even a wider smile, telling her dad that she believes it will happen. "Baby, you're getting your joy back, remember the joy of the Lord is your strength." When Odessa and her dad saw that the guard was moving in their direction, it meant that their visiting time was over. So

Odessa dad gave her a big hug and a kiss on her forehead as he said "this is not goodbye, I will see you later." Odessa said promise, and her dad said "I promise". As her dad was leaving, he told Odessa to remember "you are more than a conqueror." Then Odessa smiled a really big smile as she waved goodbye to her dad.

Later that evening, all the reporters begin to file their stories about the trial. They say that Mr. Prod may just end up sending Odessa to the gas chamber. They have been quoting Mr. Prod throughout the trial, and their favorite quote is "Mr. Prod always gets his man, but in this case his woman." They're saying Odessa doesn't even have the chance that a snowball has in hell, and at least that turns into water before it evaporates. Everyone around town knows that Mr. Prod always wins his cases. They quoted him saying, 'that he's not about to break his winning streak with this case. She is guilty and everybody knows it. My job is not to prove it, that's the defense attorney's job. My job is to quickly bring this trial to a speedy end and save the state and the taxpayers of this great state some money, end of quote."

Worldly News Tonight (WNT) anchorman Darwine Trestor is reporting in the studio on the day's current events. "From today's trial, the State of Illinois versus Odessa Princeton, we see Mr. Prod is still calling his long list of witnesses. He got caught up in a little snag today. (Some laughing in the newsroom) Once Mr. Straitway proved that Prod's witness was really an escapee from the looney farm, that turned the tables for Mr. Straightway. That was really great on Mr. Straitway's part; he now has a point on our scoreboard. (Clapping in the newsroom) Ok, Mr. Prod, get out there and do your stuff, if you're going to win you can't have any more slip-ups. And maybe you should think twice: Mr. Straitway could really be a worthy opponent. Mr. Prod remember the world is watching. We all have become such fans of Mr. Prod. We like to see him do his stuff, as he says it's his Mojo working on his behalf. (More laughter in the studio) This is Darwine Trestor from WNT saying goodnight, and be sure to tune in at this same time and station tomorrow night, for more updates on this exciting trial. Thank you for watching. Cut, that's a wrap, go to commercial."

Darwine is one of those people who are just out for prestige and power. He doesn't care who gets hurt or who he steps on to get there. He doesn't believe in God; he believes you make your own way in this life by whom you know and who you are connected to.

CHAPTER
13

It is a new day, and Odessa is up praying, with most of her prayers directed at the trial today. Odessa starts by asking God to help her and to use this trial to and for His glory. "Father please don't let the enemy to triumph over me. He doesn't have all power, you do. I need the protection of your angels every step of the way. Father, I need to know you're listening to me, please show me your intervention on today. Please stop Mr. Prod, he is prosecuting me. He is making Christians everywhere look like a joke. Please help Mr. Straitway-- he needs you in his life, and to help with my defense. I thank you in the name of Jesus the Christ."

Court is now in session and Mr. Prod is calling his first witness of the day. The bailiff called Detective Brad Rodgers to the stand. "Do you swear to tell the truth, the whole truth, so help you God?" "I do."

"Detective Rodgers, in your own words can you tell us why and what lead you to the arrest of the defendant, Odessa Princeton?"

"On Thursday March 13, 1990, I received a call about 1:35 p.m., about a possible murder at the Osbourne's estate. When I arrived, they were removing Mr. Harrington Osbourne III's body from the library. One of my officers told me that Mr. Theodore Osbourne claimed the defendant had murdered his father. I also heard him shouting it out for myself."

"Objection Your Honor."

"On what grounds Mr. Straitway?"

"Hear say."

"The jury will strike that last remarks from this witness. You may continue Detective Rodgers, and keep all your comments to a professional standpoint."

"Yes, Your Honor. I and my staff began to question the household staff. I questioned the defendant myself; she was very nervous and kind of out of it, as if in a state of shock."

"Objection Your Honor."

"On what grounds, Mr. Straitway?"

"The witness is not a doctor and he is not qualified as to say what state of mind or well-being that the defendant was in."

Judge Watts instructed the jurors to "strike the last remarks of the witness, as to the well-being and state of mind of defendant from your records. Ok detective, I am warning you, stick to the facts of the case."

"Yes, your Honor."

"Proceed."

"After questioning everyone, I felt there was enough evidence to warrant an arrest of the defendant. The defendant had a sticky substance on her hands, and later on she allowed us to take a sample of it. It was also found on the paramedic's hands that was trying to save the deceased's life. He said he got it on his hands after performing CPR on the deceased's body."

"Objection, Your Honor."

"Grounds Mr. Straitway?"

"That goes to hearsay."

"Objection, Your Honor," Mr. Prod was shouting. "Your Honor, we can call the paramedic up here to confirm this witness' testimony. The defense attorney is not allowing this witness to give or finish his testimony."

"Your Honor; can we get a ruling on my objection?"

Judge Watts was getting tired of all the objections from both sides. He asked both attorneys to approach the bench. He told both of them to hold all of their objections regarding this witness and his testimony until he was finished. Then he would rule on each objection according to its merit.

Detective Rodgers was still on the stand, trying to finish from where he had left off. "I had the sample sent to both the lab and to the coroner's office. This caused us to ask for and receive several search warrants. The search warrants were for Ms. Princeton's room at the Osbourne's estate, the defendant's resident in the city, and her vehicle, a tan 1988 Ford Explorer. In her room at the Osbourne's mansion, we found a plastic bag with patches inside in the bottom of her under garments drawer. And we also found letters about doing harm to the deceased, and a folder with a couple of the deceased's doctored up wills. They contained a lot of changes on them. They were all typed and not handwritten, but there were places that it looked as if she used a lot of correction ink. One of the wills stated that the deceased was cutting her and her church out of his will. Another one was found in her wastebasket. At her residence in the city we found more of the patches, and a threatening letter intended for the deceased in her closet in her jacket pocket. We then discovered inside the trunk of her vehicle, there under the flap inside the spare tire rim, a small bottle containing what seemed to be the same substance that was on all the patches we had recovered from both places."

Teddy was sitting in the courtroom, looking like the cat that had swallowed the canary, thinking he really did a good job on Odessa by having so much evidence planted in all those various places. He thought to himself, "no one will ever find out I paid Ned to place those letters in Odessa's jacket pocket. She is so dumb, she didn't even see me coming. Geneva is having what we call 'daydreams' and she's starting to see the day of the accident more clearly."

Mr Prod continued: "Your Honor; the prosecution would like to place these things into evidence, as Exhibits #1, #2, #3, and #4."

"So noted. The items will become evidence in this trial."

"Now detective, you said that Odessa was cut out of the deceased's will. "How did you arrive at that conclusion? Did you say that the same sticky substance was on both the defendant as well as the deceased? Please tell this court, did you find anything inside her

Bible? I thought the Bible said thou shalt not kill. But the defendant, Odessa, being a Christian would know that. Yet Odessa has found it in her heart to murder her kind, trusting, unsuspecting, and very defenseless employer. Who would have thought?"

Suddenly Mr. Teddy shouted from the back of the courtroom, 'I would and did suspect her, she murdered my father!' Suddenly the entire courtroom went into an uproar.

"Objection!" As Mr. Straitway began to stand to his feet, he repeated "objection, your Honor, Mr. Prod is baiting the witness and he's turning this court into a circus."

"Order! Order in this courtroom," shouted Judge Watts as he stuck his desk with his gavel. "Everyone sit down and please take your seats. All those still standing in the back, please sit down and take your seats! Turning to the bailiff, "please remove Mr. Osbourne from my courtroom, now! And while he is doing so, attorneys please approach the bench."

Judge Watts started off by telling Prosecutor Prod to stop with all his theatrics, and stick to questions that pertained to the alleged murder only and not the defendant's beliefs." And Attorney Straitway, I will rule on your objection as soon as we are finished here. Do we have an understanding gentleman? Because contrary to what you might believe, this is my courtroom and I don't allow circuses and there are definitely no ringmasters except me. Step back so I can rule on Mr. Straitway's objection."

Judge Watts then spoke to the entire courtroom. "I do not and will not allow my court to be disrupted with outbursts in any shape, form or fashion. If you try me, you will be arrested and found in contempt of court. And I will make sure it is followed through to the highest extent of the law. Now to the matter at hand, Attorney Straitway's objections stand. The jury will strike the last statements that Prosecutor Prod spoke from your records. Mr. Prod do you have any more questions for this witness?"

"No, Your Honor."

"Mr. Straitway, your cross."

"Detective Rodgers, did my client try to resist when you asked for the sample of the sticky substance on her hands? Let's just say, for the benefit of this court, that you have investigated lots of murders in your time. So in your expert opinion, did my client seem like she had just committed murder? Wasn't she the one they said was administering CPR before the arrival of the paramedics? You testified that my client was right there all the time. You mean she didn't try and run away from the crime scene? When you questioned her, did she ever admit to murdering the deceased or anyone else? You may answer now, Detective Rodgers."

"No, she didn't confess to me nor any of my staff. She agreed to let us take the sample, stating it wasn't on her hands before she started giving the deceased CPR. All she did was declare her innocence, and didn't understand why she was being accused of murder. She pointed out to all of us that the deceased, her employer and friend, had just been declared DOA."

"So detective please answer me this, why and how could it be murder? From what you are telling me and the court, it seemed as if she was really trying to understand and trying to grasp it all. Your Honor, I have no more questions for this witness."

"Mr. Prod redirect?"

"No, Your Honor."

Judge Watts, looking at the witness, said "you may step down. Mr. Prod you may call your next witness."

"Your Honor the prosecution will now call Coroner Trixion to the stand."

Coroner Scott Trixion has been answering lot of questions from Prosecutor Prod. "Your Honor, we would like to place into evidence the coroner's report as exhibit #5."

"So noted," said the judge.

"Now can you tell this court if the sticky substance that was found on the body is the very same that was found on the defendant's hand? Did they contain some type of poison? In your report, your findings show you were you able to pin down the type of poison, and how it works. Finally were you able to determine if it was what caused the deceased's death?"

The Coroner said the sticky substance found on both was an exact match. "It was my office's finding that the deceased was poisoned, and he died from a lethal overdose of it. This poison that was used is called calcium hydroxide." Stepping away, Mr. Prod said "I have no more questions for this witness." The judge said, "your cross, Mr. Straitway."

The first thing Mr. Straitway asked Coroner Trixion was "how were you able to determine that is what killed the deceased with such a small amount? And were you further able to determine how much of that particular poison it would take to kill a person? And how soon after it enters the body would death occur? You said there were large amounts of the poison found the deceased's organs. Were you able to determine why it took the poison so long to kill the deceased? How is was possible, if there were only small amounts of that poison found on the patches? In your expert opinion is there any other way that such a large amount could've gotten into the deceased's body? Could the deceased mistakenly do this-- could he have taken it on his own? How can one give this type of poison to anyone without it being detected? How long does it take for the poison to take effect and what type of symptoms or side effects would one look for?"

Trying to answer him, the coroner said, "my report is still inconclusive as to how so much poison was found in the deceased body or how it got there in such a high dose. The patches that were tagged from the defendant's home, had such a small amount on them, we barely had enough to analyze. That type of poison is odorless and tasteless. The deceased could have been receiving doses of it for months without detection. As I said in my report, our findings were, and my staff and I weren't able to retrieve enough samples to determine how long the deceased had been being poisoned."

"Your Honor, I have no more questions for this witness."

"Redirect, Mr. Prod?"

"No, your Honor."

Directing his comment to the witness, the judge said "you may step down." Continuing on, Judge Watts stated "due to the lateness of the hour, this court will reconvene tomorrow morning at ten o'clock. All stand, and then this court is adjoined. We will reconvene at 10 a.m. tomorrow morning."

As Judge Watts was walking away from his bench, he looked at it as if in some state of disbelief. He was reminded of his dreams, wondering what they have to do with this particular case. Shaking his head, Judge Watts left the courtroom.

On the evening news coverage of the trial, several reporters are saying Mr. Prod better be careful, because Mr. Straitway doesn't look like he's just going to sit still and let him crucify his client. Mr. Straitway really defended her well today, and looks like Mr. Prod is coming up a little short.

Back at WNT, they've been discussing the trial as well. "What kind of stuff was going on in that courtroom today? One would think it really was a circus. You see how mad Judge Watts got? Mr. Prod better watch out-- there is a new judge in town and he is not accepting any crazy stuff going on during this trial. There will be no horse and pony show as in the past trials that we have come to love to watch. Does this mean Mr. Prod is going to have to play nice, or what?" Showing the tape of everyone exiting the courtroom, one reporter noticed something. "Did you see how the judge looked back before leaving the courtroom?" Co-anchor Veronica Best spoke out, "Yeah did you see that, when they were leading Odessa out of the courtroom? Why did they have four county Sheriff's deputies guarding her? Did she attempt to escape or try to commit suicide? That poor woman, I bet she's under a lot of pressure." Darwine turned to her and whispered, "Veronica do you have any idea what are you talking about? There were only two sheriffs with her." Right then Mr. Lester Booche, the TV station manager, said "cut-- go to commercial. Darwine Trestor announced they were taking a short commercial break, they would be right back, and to stay tuned for more updates on today's trial.

No sooner than they went to commercial, Mr. Booche started screaming at Veronica, asking what hell was she talking about? She said "didn't you see the four sheriffs on the tape?"

"No, and you didn't either," he bellowed as he showed her the excerpts from Odessa leaving the courtroom. Everyone in the station started whispering among themselves. Mr. Booche told Veronica to go get a drink of water and get back before the break is over. "And once you get back in that chair Veronica, you be as quiet as a church mouse unless you see your name on that screen. Have I made myself clear?"

"Yes sir," she muttered as she walked off to get herself something to drink. Veronica began to question herself. "I did see four sheriffs at first. Someone must have edited the tape and cut the other two out. But how and why would anyone do that? Does someone here have it in for me?"

Veronica is a saved Christian, but no one at her job is aware of it. It's not that she's hiding it, but she hasn't made it of public record either. She flows in the gift of discernment, but she doesn't understand everything about it. She just knows she sometimes sees things that are not there to the natural eye. Veronica feels they may not take her seriously if they knew this about her at her workplace. Well, after that outburst they just may never take her seriously. She has worked for WNT for over fifteen years, working very hard to become co-anchor. Veronica knows that it was God that helped her.

Just then she heard Darwine calling her, laughing "I know you're not trying to hide after that outburst. Come on and face your, rather my, public and follow my lead, and mine only!" Darwine started by welcoming the audience back. "Thanks for staying tuned in to our station WNT. Hey wasn't that some kind of funny outburst from my co-anchor Veronica Best? She really had you going didn't she? Don't feel bad-- she had me going as well. Did you all think that Prosecutor Prod was the only one who could pull off a great and memorable stunt? Well, that was just a stunt we at the station cooked up just to see if everyone was really paying attention to us. I know that you are, because a few of you called in during that commercial break. We at WNT just want to say thank you to all our fans and supporters out there. Now back to that trial, huh. Did everyone get a load of Attorney Straitway in his cross of both of Prosecutor Prod's witnesses? He was great wasn't he? (Applauding in the station) Mr. Straitway did his homework. Well it is time for us to say goodnight. This is anchor Darwine Trestor coming to you live each evening from WNT. We'll see you again tomorrow night at this same time and station. Again thanks, especially to those that called in earlier. Please continue listening and keep us tuned in. We love you all, here at WNT, Worldly News Tonight."

"Goodnight. Cut it a wrap," shouted Mr. Booche, "go to the next program it's about to start, we ran a little over our time."

"Veronica I need to see you back in my office, right now!" Mr. Booche was shouting. Veronica was nervous, but she whispered a prayer and then reported to Mr. Booche in his office. "Veronica, do you need a vacation or some time off? Just say something before you go blabbing everything out across the airways. I believed we were able to smooth it over well, don't you?"

"Yes sir, Mr. Booche. I believe everyone truly thought we had pulled a stunt like Darwine said. First Mr. Booche, I would truly like to apologize for my outburst. I really did believe I saw four county sheriff's deputies with her."

He said "maybe you should take a few days off with pay and get checked out."

"I'm alright, sir. I don't need to take any time off."

Mr. Booche kept on talking as if he hadn't even heard Veronica speaking to him. "… then come back fresh and well rested with a new perspective on the case, maybe even a different angle that we can approach from. You are good at your job; now take the days off and I'll see you when you return. Veronica said "okay l will;" then she went and got all her belongings and left the station.

Mr. Lester Booche has been the manager and owner of station WNT for sixteen years. He is under a lot of pressure to get the story out about the trial. Mr. Booche has always been all about business, and only business. He doesn't have time for foolishness through trial and error. This trial has too many twists and turns for him. Mr. Booche just likes everything to run smoothly. He was beginning to question what he believes and the people around him; especially his workers. He likes for everything to be wrapped up all tightly and very neat at the end of the day, or there will be a lot of heads rolling because Mr. Booche will not be placing his head on the chopping block for the incompetence of others.

Mr. Brice is the private eye Mr. Harrington Osbourne III hired a little over ten years ago to find out the truth about Rebecca and her husband Freddrick's deaths. The accident report said it was proven to only be an accident. But Mr. Osbourne never believed it was an accident. He always felt someone had murdered his little girl, and he wasn't about to let them get away with it. So he searched for the best P.I in his or her field, and that's how he came to know and hired Mr. Brice.

For years there had been very little communication between the two of them. Every time Mr. Brice had a lead, it would somehow lead to a dead end. But, Mr. Osbourne always said he believed in Mr. Brice and if anyone could find out what happened, he would be the one. So every month he would send a payment directly to Mr. Brice's account, so that he would stay on the case. Mr. Osbourne always told Mr. Brice "we have come such a long way. We are really close, and we can't stop now. The trial is still warm and smelly; you just have to pick up its scent again." Mr. Brice had already found the Good Samaritan that helped pull Geneva to safety, and he had talked to both the officer and the paramedic from the car accident. Besides them, Mr. Brice had had a long conversation with the county mechanic about the brakes on Freddrick's car. He said they could have been tampered with, but at the time they didn't have enough evidence to prove or disprove it.

Then one day, to his surprise Mr. Brice heard something about a man being arrested for the attempted murder of his sister in law. Now it seemed that the tides were turning in their favor. As Mr. Brice looked into it further the man had the same name as the mechanic that disappeared from the Osbourne's estate. Chester Browning had left a few days before the deadly accident, with no forwarding address-- not even for his last paycheck. "If that wasn't suspicious, I don't know what is. That was no coincidence; he had to be the same person," Brice thought to himself. Chester had tried "fixing" his sister-in-law's car brakes as well, but she survived. When they told Chester's wife that her sister's brakes had malfunctioned, she immediately reported Chester to the authorities. Once Mr. Brice was able to reach the sister in law, he took a trip down to Ohio. He met with Chester about the accident that killed Rebecca Osbourne- Trice. At first, Chester denied knowing anything about it, but once a reward--

money-- was mentioned he started singing just enough to keep Mr. Brice interested. Chester told Mr. Brice that he knew about it and who all was in on it. Then Chester said if he and Mr. Osbourne wanted any more details, they had to post his bond, and if they didn't he would develop a quick case of amnesia. Chester also said that he was in need a top notch lawyer to get him off, because he was afraid the state of Ohio was going to give him the death penalty. So Chester wanted the lawyer, a written and signed statement that no one would ever file charges against him in Rebecca's accident case, and fifty thousand dollars in cash. Once Chester was assured of getting just what he asked for from Mr. Osbourne, he would name names. Upon further discussion with Mr. Osbourne, he and Chester came to an agreement. Mr. Osbourne wired the money to an account so Mr. Brice could oversee it all until the very end. Mr. Osbourne knew that his Rebecca had been murdered, and he was going to finally find out who was behind it all, and why. Mr. Osbourne also planned to have the responsible parties arrested for Rebecca and Freddrick's murders and the attempted murder of his precious granddaughter Geneva. If Geneva only knew how much her grandfather really loved her, and how long he had waited to get some kind of closure, as well as justice for their murders.

Mr. Brice was supposed to tell Mr. Osbourne everything he had found out that following Friday, March 17, 1989. Upon arriving in town, Mr. Brice soon found out that Mr. Osbourne had died... or was he really murdered, like his daughter?

That Wednesday evening, Mr. Brice and Mr. Osbourne discussed solving yet another possible case: his own murder. Mr. Osbourne informed him of some of his findings and said "if anything happens to me, I believe I have concrete evidence on who would have murdered me. I have left you a trail of breadcrumbs, well the whole loaf," Mr. Osbourne laughed. "I have confidence in you, Mr. Brice, that you will be able to solve this one very quickly and make sure they pay, and pay dearly!"

After Mr. Osbourne had his conversation with Mr. Brice, he called Mr. Johns and said he had received some strong and very incriminating information pertaining Rebecca's so called accident.

Mr. Osbourne informed Mr. Johns of some immediate changes he wanted made to his will, and he wanted to have everything finalized by Friday morning. He told Mr. Johns he expected him to be quick about it and very discreet. Once Mr. Osbourne finished talking to Mr. Johns, he called for his friend and trusted butler, Oscar. Mr. Osbourne gave him some things to do for him before he retired for the evening. Mr. Osbourne told Oscar that they would have a further discussion during lunch on tomorrow. It turned out to be the day of Mr. Osbourne death.

Mr. Brice is back in town and has finally contacted Lisa and scheduled a place and time to meet. He instructed her to bring him everything that she had found. When he opened the envelope addressed to Odessa, everything he and Mr. Osbourne had previously talked about started to make sense. Mr. Brice questioned Lisa about how the trial was going, what was the name of Odessa's attorney, and does Odessa feel that Mr. Straitway was doing a good job representing her? They talked for about an hour. Mr. Brice didn't tell Lisa what he had read or what he was going to do with all the information that she had given him. He just told Lisa he would take care of everything, and to tell Odessa don't worry about anything, and don't mention anything about him to anybody. Lisa left and Mr. Brice started to set some things in motion. The wheels in his head had already started to turn. Ned was the next person on his list to find and talk to. Then Mr. Brice could set his net in the right spot and see how many crooks will step into it. They will be falling into yet another one of his and the late Mr. Osbourne's very well laid traps.

CHAPTER
14

PROSECUTOR PROD HAS CALLED Teddy to the stand. The bailiff said "this court now calls Mr. Theodore Osbourne to the stand. Place your right hand on this Bible. Do you swear to tell the truth, the whole truth, and nothing but the truth so help you God?"

"I do."

"State your name for the record."

"My name is Theodore Osbourne, but my friends call me Teddy. You can call me Teddy as well."

"Okay, so Teddy how are you, or are you in any way related to the deceased?"

"He was my father and she murdered him!" Teddy yelled as he was pointing to Odessa

"Objection, Your Honor. No one here has proven that a murder has been committed, to my knowledge or to this court."

Judge Watts said "the recorder will strike that from the records, and the jurors are instructed to disregard the witness' last remark. Mr. Osbourne, please stick to the question at hand and only answer what is asked of you. Do you understand?"

"Yes, your Honor."

"Mr. Prod you may continue with your examination."

"How do you know the defendant?"

"She worked for my father as his nurse, and only God knows what else she was trying to be."

"Objection, your Honor!!"

"Mr. Osbourne, now let me warn you, and let this be my last warning to you: Only answer the questions that you have been asked of you. If you continue on with the way you have been going, you will find yourself in contempt of my court. Have I made myself clear?"

"Yes, sir, Your Honor."

"Mr. Prod, you may continue."

"Did you know if your father had changed his will?"

"Yes, and he confided in me that Odessa was pressuring him to make sure that she was left in his will."

"Objection! That goes to hearsay."

"Sustained. The last remark will be stricken from these court proceedings. The jury will omit that last remark. Mr. Prod instruct your witness to answer to what he has been privileged to, and only him; not anyone else."

"So, Teddy. How much of your father's estate was he leaving to the defendant, if anything?"

"I don't really know. He was always changing his will. Did the defendant know that she was in his will? Was she at all aware that she had been cut out of his will, and that she wasn't going to receive nothing, not even one red penny? Yes, she did. My father said he was going to leave all his investments to Geneva, and when he changed it she killed him!"

When Geneva heard this in the courtroom she couldn't believe her ears. "What was Uncle Teddy talking about? Why was he lying on the witness stand? Is he telling the truth? Then what about all those wills that I saw lying around? Were they real, or was it all a plant to set me up? Is Odessa really innocent? I need some answers; I need to know what has really been going on. And who did really murder my grandfather and why? What have I done?" Crying she walked out of the courtroom.

"Objection, your Honor. That goes to hearsay."

"Mr. Osbourne, you are now trying the court's patience. So if I were you, I would not want to be warned again! Mr. Prod control your witnesses or else this court will!"

"Teddy, did she know where your father kept his important papers?"

"Yes, she did. Everyone in the house knew he kept them in his safe."

"Do you know if and when she ever saw the changed will?"

"No, but…"

"Your Honor I have no more questions for this witness."

"Attorney Straitway, your cross."

"Not at this time, your Honor, but the defense reserves the right to call this witness at a later date during this trial. And to treat him as a hostile witness, with the understanding that the prosecutor may redirect."

"Prosecutor Prod please call your next witness."

Teddy was very nervous as he stepped down out of the witness box. He had seen Geneva leave the courtroom during his testimony. How was he going to smooth this over? He'd better start thinking of something pretty darn fast. Geneva hasn't been herself since that first day of the trial.

"The Prosecution calls Mr. Markus Johns to the stand." After he had been sworn in, Prod asked "Mr. Johns please tell this court what your profession is."

"I am an attorney and licensed in the state of Illinois to practice law."

"How long have you been practicing law?"

"For a little over eighteen years."

"Did you know the deceased, and if so how did you know him?"

"Yes, I knew and worked for Mr. Harrington Osbourne, III. I was his attorney for over seventeen years, right up until the day he was murdered on March 16, 1989."

"Objection, Your Honor, it has not yet been proven that the deceased was murdered."

"Sustained. Please refrain from using the word 'murdered', until someone proves that the deceased was truly murdered. Do we have an understanding?"

"Yes, your Honor."

"Mr. Johns it was stated in earlier testimony by the deceased's son that his father had made changes to his will, in which the deceased had apparently cut the defendant out of it. Is this true? Were you aware of this, and how are you privy to such information?"

"Yes I am, and I was aware that Mr. Osbourne had changed his will, and that the defendant was cut out of it. I know this because being his attorney, I was the one who he had to make the necessary changes to his will. Which I did at his request."

"Did the deceased tell you that he feared for his life? Was he afraid of the defendant?"

"Yes, he had a real concern for his life. He called me late that Wednesday evening, the day before his death, and told me the changes he was making could get him killed." The courtroom went into a loud hush.

"Did the deceased name who he felt would harm him?"

"Yes, he named the defendant. I asked Mr. Osbourne did he still want to still do this, he said yes and have the changes done by Friday. I asked him why doesn't he just fire Odessa, but he said he wanted to give her a chance to find another job before he terminated her employment."

"So, you're saying that the deceased couldn't let the defendant go because he was at her mercy?"

"Yes, that about sums it all up in a nutshell."

Straightway jumped in immediately. "Objection, your Honor. Hearsay, calls for conclusion and speculation on the witness part."

Prosecutor Prod was still examining the witness, as if he didn't hear the objection. "Are you saying that the deceased kept her on in his employment even though he knew she was planning to kill or rather murder him?"

"Objection your Honor, leading the witness, goes to speculation."

"Sustained on both counts, the jury will disregard the last two questions from the prosecutor and the last two answers from the witness. Prosecutor Prod I suggest that you tread lightly because this court's indulgence and patience is growing very thin. I would highly recommend you stay in the boundaries that this court has set, or you and your witness will find yourself in contempt of this court. Am

I making myself clear, sirs?" Both Prosecutor Prod and Mr. Johns chimed in, "yes Your Honor, we're clear." Mr. Prod was just standing there for a few minutes, and then the judge asked him did he have any more questions for this witness? He answered "no your Honor, I don't have any more questions for this witness." Then the judge said "your cross, Mr. Straitway."

"Your Honor the defense has no questions for this witness at this time but we do reserve the right to call him later on in this trial."

"So noted. Bailiff what time is it?"

"It is four forty five, Your Honor."

Judge Watts, in response to the time, said "it's later than I thought it was. So this court will be in recess until Monday morning. We will reconvene and meet back here at 10 a.m. sharp."

Odessa asked Mr. Straitway why he didn't question them both, seeing that they were lying and everyone could see it. "No, everyone couldn't see that they were lying. You have to relax and trust me. We will expose them for who they are and what they did. Now you just keep praying and leave the rest up to me, okay?" As Mr. Straitway smiled at her, she smiled back at him and said "Okay." Then Mr. Straitway said "I will see you before court starts on Monday."

That evening Mr. Brice met with Judge Watts in his chambers. Mr. Brice showed Judge Watts all the information he had concerning the trial. The judge was taken back; this wasn't just about one murder it was about three and one attempted murder. The judge asked Mr. Brice what he planned to do with his findings. Mr. Brice said he had set up a meeting with the defense attorney Mr. Straitway for a meeting of the minds. The judge agreed that would be best for everyone concerned.

Mr. Brice arrived early at the meeting place that he had sat up with Mr. Straitway. Mr. Straitway was running late for the meeting; besides, he didn't really know what a private eye had to do with his defense. When he arrived Mr. Brice was having coffee, and he asked if Mr. Straitway wanted a cup? Mr. Straitway said "yes I take it black with two sugars," then Mr. Brice called the waitress over and she poured him a cup. Mr. Straitway was very eager to know what this meeting was all about, so he just asked. "Mr. Brice said do you mind if I order something to eat before we get started? I have been driving nonstop to get here for these two meetings."

"No I don't, I guess I will get something too, since I told Mae Helen not to hold dinner for me."

"Who is Mae Helen, may I ask?"

"Oh," laughing as he answered "Mae Helen is my wife, and she's a darn good cook. I hope the food here is just as tasty."

"Well, I don't think it will be as good as your wife's, but I believe they will come in a close second." Once they had placed their orders, Mr. Brice began to explain why he asked for this meeting. He showed Mr. Straitway all of his findings. This was just what Mr. Straitway needed to win this case. Mr. Straitway started feeling that he had been dealt a better hand. Why, this news is what they would call his "ace in the hole." Mr. Straitway said "Odessa told me that she was innocent. She's always telling me she didn't know why they were calling it murder, then on top of that charging her with it; that's all she has been saying since the first day I met her. Odessa said she and the deceased were good friends."

"Now do you believe that she has been telling you the truth all this time?"

"Yes, I do now; I should have believed her because she's been declaring her innocence to anyone and everyone who would listen. And don't forget, her trust and faith in her God, it is so strong."

Mr. Brice said "I know, I have heard about it from a few people and it's unshakeable."

"So how do you propose we do this?"

"After we finish going over all this evidence, you just add me to your witness list and I will get the party started. We're going to have ourselves a big barn fire you know, because we have a lot of foxes to catch, and strip. Don't you agree it is time for payday! Both Mr. Brice and Mr. Straitway started laughing, but they were very serious as well.

On his way from the meeting, Mr. Straitway knew that had a lot to consider. He had to figure out his lineup of witnesses, and also his line of questioning for each of them. He had received the evidence that was going to blow this case wide open, and the other one as well. He said "well there goes my weekend fishing trip. Maybe Mae Helen will still be up when I get home. I know she will be so surprised to see and hear about what I have learned. I just know she will be excited for Odessa, and of course she will make sure I thank God for helping with this case."

Yes, Mae Helen was up and watching the late night news. "Hey, honey, look: you're just in time to hear what that Darwine has to say about the trial today." They went to a commercial break. "Awe, Mae Helen, you know I don't care what they say, they all think that Mr. Prod is going to win. Hush it's on, sit down and take a seat, we'll talk when it's over."

"Good Evening, this is anchor Darwine Trestor, and tonight we have with us Henry Banks, sitting in for co-anchor Veronica Best. (Applauding in the studio) Well I know that you all have been anxiously waiting for today's trial updates, so let's just get right to it. Prosecutor Prod called the deceased's son, Teddy, to the stand today. He told everyone that the defendant murdered his father because Mr. Osbourne changed his will. He also said his father was leaving his investments to someone named Geneva. Who is this Geneva person and how does she fit into everything? (He was saying this as he was looking and digging through some papers in front of him.) Oh, I have it here, Geneva is the deceased's granddaughter. Well, that clears that up for us all. Okay, on to the prosecution's next witness of the day. They called the deceased's attorney, Mr. Markus Johns to the stand. He verified that the deceased had changed his will, or should we say wills. He claimed that the deceased was doing this all because he feared for his life. He said he asked the deceased why he didn't fire the defendant. He said the deceased told him he was keeping her on until she (The defendant) could find employment elsewhere. Just look at what happens to you when you are nice to someone. They just take advantage and murder you. That's what both the deceased man's son and attorney said today on the stand, and we all know that they were both under oath. None of this looks good for the defendant's side. Did you all get a load of the defense attorney, Mr. Straitway, how he came out swinging with all those objections. He really seems to know how to play in the big leagues. And check this out, Judge Watts ruled in his favor on every one of them. So, why didn't Mr. Straitway, do his cross examination of each of these witnesses? What is he waiting for? He had a great opportunity to go after them while the judge is ruling in his favor. Don't they teach that in law school? It would seem as if they would. Ok, Mr. Straitway, next time just go for straight for the jugular, because given the same home court advantage, Mr. Prod will do so without any hesitation on his part. This is Darwine Trestor and our stand in co-anchor Henry Banks, who is sitting in for our beautiful co-anchor Veronica Best in her absence, saying goodnight. Have a great weekend, and please tune in again for more updates of the exciting trial. We look forward to see you at this same station and time in just three days, on Monday evening. Again, goodnight from all of us at WNT, Worldly News Tonight."

After the news went off, Mae Helen said "now what was the great emergency had to run off to that you missed dinner. Did you eat?"

"Yes I did, but it wasn't your cooking and it didn't even come close to yours." Barry told Mae Helen about his meeting with Mr. Brice and all the evidence that he had given to him. "Now I know that we can win this case. Mae Helen, you knew that Odessa was telling the truth all the time. She really didn't have anything to do with Mr. Osbourne's death. They framed her, but thanks be…"

Mae Helen interjected right away, finishing his thought "… to God. God is the only one that has the last say in every situation. I told you from the start to take the case and that He would help you prove that child's innocence. Well I guess your fishing trip is off; you did call the guys and say you can't make it, didn't you? Besides, even if you didn't, I called their wives and they will give them the message."

"Oh, Mae Helen, I would've done it myself."

"Yeah, and it's late and they've already gone to bed. Remember, you all rise up at three in the morning to go catch some poor old unsuspecting fish."

"What kind of talk is that Mae Helen? When I bring them home, you always clean, cook and eat them, just like I do."

"That may be true, but I'm not the one going out there in the dark, tricking them with those fake worms you guys use to catch them."

"Well when the guys come back with their catch, and ask if we would like some, I'll be sure and tell them 'no thank you.'"

"No you will not Barry, (As she was rubbing the top of his head that has started balding) I didn't say I didn't want any." Then they both started laughing and went on to bed for the night.

CHAPTER
15

Mr. Straitway knew he needed to get up pretty early as well. Barry had to go over the evidence again, and he needed to get all his questions written down for each witness.

Back at the mansion, Uncle Teddy had tried to smooth things over with Geneva. Teddy told her that their attorney, Mr. Johns, had just given him that information before he was called to testify. "Don't you remember seeing us talking in the hallway, over in that corner? That's what we were talking about before court started." Geneva nodded yes, but she wasn't convinced. She just wanted to get away from her uncle; she felt there were a lot of things that Uncle Teddy was hiding from her, mainly the truth.

Once Geneva finished eating dinner with her uncle, she asked to be excused, telling Teddy that with all the stuff going on with the trial today, it has made her very tired and she needed to get some rest. In her room, lying across her bed, Geneva hears her parents talking. She tried real hard to be very quiet and still so she could hear and understand them. Her mom was talking to her dad while she was packing their clothes the day of their family vacation. Her mom said "I don't know how Teddy is going to feel, seeing that dad is leaving it all to her. He probably thinks that he's giving it to you or me." They both laughed, "won't Teddy be surprised at who really gets everything." Geneva thought her mom was referring to Odessa. Maybe Uncle Teddy was right about Odessa, and grandfather was leaving everything to her. Somehow that really just didn't set well with her, and besides that it just didn't feel right. She tried to hear the more of their conversation but she fell into a deep sleep. Right back into that dream from the day of the accident.

In the dream Geneva can finally see and hear everything about the day her parents died. It all started when she was in the library with her grandfather. That's where she would spend most of her free time as a child. Grandfather always talked to her about the family business, and how "one day it will all be yours." Grandfather always played games with her, but somehow, they were all geared toward the family trucking business. She loved to hide under her grandfather's desk (even during his board meetings), so no one could find her. Her grandfather always knew where to find her, but that little secret was between the both of them only. Her grandfather always said she had a good head on her shoulders, but mainly for business. He told Geneva "one day this will all be yours." Just then she woke up, trying to collect her thoughts. She remembered that was the very day that grandfather gave her that set of model trucks and asked what were her thoughts about them. Her reply was "one thing is for sure: they are too small for us to ride in." Her grandfather began to laugh so hard that Geneva started to laugh too. "Wow," she thought "those were the good old days." She tried remembering some more but she fell back to sleep.

It's early Saturday morning, and Odessa is all washed up and dressed, ready for the day to begin. She's supposed to have a few visitors today. She's already prayed, and she has an excitement down on the inside but she doesn't know why she feels this way. She just knows that she can't wait to see her dad and aunt. Lisa said she would be there about three in the afternoon. She had a lot of questions for her, concerning the letters and all.

Mr. Straitway has been up since before dawn. He has been figuring out his witness line up. He called Doris and she will help him with his line of questions over lunch. They must be prepared for anything and everything, seeing as they are dealing with some very sensitive information.

Geneva got up very early today. Her plans were to have breakfast and leave before everyone else got up. Frankly, she was trying to avoid her Uncle Teddy at all cost, not wanting to have a confrontation with him, and definitely not wanting to hear any more of his lies. Geneva left, drove down to the stables, and parked her car out of sight so no one would see where she had gone. Lying down in the hay in one of the empty stalls, she tried very hard to figure out what happened to her parents. Then she felt like she was hearing her grandfather's voice, off in a distance like an echo, reminding her that "one day this will all be yours." "So I'm the one mother was referring to when she was talking to my dad about that day she was packing our things for our annual family vacation. We went on a vacation every year that I could remember. My parents knew Uncle Teddy didn't know who grandfather was leaving it all to. Somehow they had sensed his anger and hostility toward them. From what Geneva was starting to piece together in her thoughts, they must have felt Teddy would try and do something about it, or even better, have it done. Uncle Teddy must have thought grandfather was giving the business to my parents, maybe that's why they are dead. He didn't know at that time, but he certainly has done his homework since then. And Teddy has had time to make himself aware of everything concerning grandfather's will. Why did it take me all these years later to see him? He did say everything was left to me on the stand yesterday, didn't he? He knew that all the time, but what was with all the secrets and lies? He made me feel like I would be broke when grandfather died if we (rather, I) didn't help him to dispose of grandfather. He made up all those lies to get me to go along with him. I trusted Uncle Teddy, now I don't know what to believe, or what he is capable of doing to me. Especially now, since I'm perhaps the only one that's standing in his way of the family business."

All of Odessa's visitors came to see her that day. She enjoyed seeing her Aunt Greta-- she came with her dad and they made lots of jokes. They kept her laughing and in stitches all the time they were there. By the time Lisa came, she was all pooped out. They talked about Mr. Brice, and Lisa told her what he had said to tell her. She said she finally got the apartment all cleaned up and back in order. Lisa said "I never knew you had so much stuff in your bedroom. Where in the world did you get it all from? And please tell me how you were able hide it all without me noticing it?" They started laughing really loud. The guard on duty walked over to their table asked them to pipe down on the noise. That made them laugh as well. Then the guard came right back, and said the very same thing, only this time kind of in a threatening tone. Concerned for her friend, Lisa told Odessa she felt that maybe they should be a little quieter. Odessa, taking heed to what Lisa had said, decided that they should end the visit on a good note. They hugged and said a prayer for Odessa's continued safety and Lisa's safe return home. Then they both left the waiting room.

Tonight when Geneva went to sleep, the dream picked right back up where it had left off. They were all singing, when all of sudden her father said "Rebecca, you know he's mad at me because of your father's decision. Teddy should have never caused your father to choose, you know that I would never come between the two of them. But Teddy is always pressuring or doing crazy things he knows that your father doesn't like. Then he really gets your father upset when he pulls those power plays. I wouldn't be surprised if Teddy tried to kill you, or me, or the both of us. Then Rebecca said "Freddrick you are talking and sounding like a crazy man yourself. We both know that Teddy is crazy, but I don't think he is that treacherous, do you? Freddrick, slow down-- you're going kind of fast." Then there was a silence, until Freddrick shouted, "Rebecca, something is wrong with the brakes". Still shouting, with a panic in his voice, "I can't stop or slow down." Freddrick was saying that as he was driving and turning into one of the curves. Rebecca told him to calm down and press on the brakes a little harder. Geneva was getting upset in the back seat, and started asking both of her parents what was wrong. Her dad's response was "I think Teddy has found a way to get rid of both of us." Rebecca said "Teddy has gone and killed us; even his only niece that he claims to love so much. Geneva started to cry, so Rebecca started trying to get her seat belt unfastened so she could see about her. All while she was still hollering for Freddrick to keep pressing down on the brakes and to please keep his eyes on the road. Then everything went blank for Geneva. All she remembers from there is waking up in the hospital one morning, some three and a half months later, asking for her parents only to find out they had died. She also remembered feeling all alone, with no remembrance of that deadly dreadful day.

Waking up now, with the truth after all these years, Geneva just laid in the haystack crying. Uncle Teddy was somehow responsible for the murder of her parents and now "I have helped him commit yet another one. I helped Uncle Teddy murder the only other person in the world that really loved me." Geneva started trying to figure out how she could right her wrongs. She really wished it was Monday already, but it was still only Saturday night. Well, she still had a day or two to figure out just what she was going to do to set everything right, but at what cost? That was not a luxury that she possessed at this time. She really couldn't afford to let her uncle get away any longer; "he must pay for what he has done, even if I go down with him."

Hours later, a very tired Mr. Straitway has continued to work very hard all day and way into the evening. He and Doris were preparing his line of questions for the trial on Monday morning. He doesn't know how many more witnesses the prosecution is going to call, but he wants to be ready whenever they rest. He has his list of witnesses lined up. He feels it will take a couple of days, but it will be well worth it. Stopping just for a moment, he whispered a prayer of thanks and gratitude to the Lord for all His help. Then he asked God to please help him to stay humble, and not to be prideful like Mr. Prod. Straitway knew that if he was to win this case, it would put him in a different league all together. He would have more cases, especially the big cases, which means more money and power and more of your name and face in the limelight. Barry wanted that, but he didn't want it at the expense of his marriage and his family. Barry had watched it destroy so many of his colleague's lives and practices. He loves his wife and his family, and now he's learning more to love, trust, lean, and rely on God for himself. This has been a hard thing for Barry in the past, but dealing with this trial and Odessa has caused him to rethink his place, and his belief in God. Barry has had to go back to his foundational teachings. He is no longer afraid of what lies in waiting for him but "Who" will be waiting for him when it is all said and done. This is not because of the evidence or Mr. Brice, it's because he has rediscovered his first love. It is a wonderful feeling to know if you are being persecuted anywhere for anything, God is there and He is always listening and watching for your response.

Barry retires after a long day of working. He goes and takes his bubble bath (he likes to take them when he's troubled and or he needs really to unwind and relax) so he can get a good night's rest.

CHAPTER
16

It's Sunday morning, and Odessa is wide awake, filled with more excitement than ever, and thanking God for His many blessings and His protection. She knows that He will intervene on her behalf. But no matter how long it might take, she is willing and going to be His light shining very brightly for Him. She began praying for everyone around her and asking God to help them personally and with their situations that brought them to this place. She prayed, "Father, I know that you know all things, and I know that you can help them and me, please show yourself to them in a mighty way. Give them a glimpse that they will never forget. Show them and cause them to experience your love. I seal this prayer and all prayers that I pray, in the name of your darling son Jesus the Christ."

Odessa read her Bible for a long time, and then she heard the guards picking up and dropping off food trays. She hadn't even touched her breakfast and now it was lunch time. She passed her tray to the guard in exchange for her lunch tray. Her lunch looked and smelled inviting, but Odessa wasn't sure about it once she tasted it. She ate it because she knew she had to keep up her strength. After Odessa finished all her lunch, she started thinking about her friend Mr. O, and how he would make her laugh. Odessa and Mr. O had a lot of fun together, and she missed their talks before his bedtime. She tried to picture her family and friends at church; oh how she would love to be in their midst one more time, singing and praising God for all He has done. Then Odessa started singing the song 'I will rejoice and be glad'. As Odessa sang the words of that song, she could feel the presence of the Lord. With tears running down her face, She began to pray for every life that has touched her life. Odessa knew that is what the heart of God was really about: souls. Then She went to her Bible to read Numbers 23: 19. She knew that scripture by heart but she wanted not only to read it but to see God's promises in His Word. By the time the singing and praising was done it was now Odessa's dinner time. She said "my how time flies."

Lying on her bed after dinner, Odessa began to reflect on the trial. She hadn't seen Mr. Straitway that weekend. At first he was her only visitor, but never in Odessa's wildest dreams did she think she would ever be missing him. Now she is not only missing him, but now she's looking forward to his visit. Mr. Straitway had promised he would see her before they went back to court. While she was in thought, the guard said she had a visitor. Odessa began to hurry up, fixing her hair and her clothes to go to the visiting room.

Teddy hasn't seen much of Geneva this weekend, and now it's Sunday evening. He's still been trying to find Chester to no avail. Teddy feels that maybe if he can't find him with all his connections and resources, no one will find Chester. So now Teddy's breathing with a little sigh of relief, he feels all is good on his end.

Teddy ringed for Oscar to bring his dinner, but Pierre the cook came with his meal instead. Teddy asked him where was Oscar; Pierre told him Oscar had handed in his two weeks' notice of resignation about three weeks ago. "Surely he gave you a copy as well. Oscar finished moving all of his belongings out Friday while you were at the court." Teddy said, "I'm glad he's gone, and good riddance to bad rubbish. I never expected him to stay as long as he did after my father was murdered. I never trusted him, and I don't know what my father ever saw in him. Oscar was always lurking in places he shouldn't have been. Then he had the nerve to be walking around here like he owned the place. I'm glad Oscar left us on his own, because it would've only been a short time before our paths crossed and I would have had to fire him. Now he is free to go somewhere else and bug the heck out of them instead of me. And just where did Oscar go, Pierre, did he tell you? I want to send him his last check so that he never has a reason to show back up here."

Pierre said he hadn't a clue, he also said they never really talked, outside of Oscar giving him the list of meals to prepare for his father each day. "Oscar really wasn't close to any of the staff, except for Odessa maybe, I saw them laughing together once or twice. She was the closest one to him, that I might even say she could have been his friend, maybe his only one." Then Teddy dismissed him, and he began to eat his dinner. Somehow he wasn't able to enjoy it. He kept hearing "they might have been friends" playing over and over in his head. Is that why Oscar said that he didn't want to testify for the prosecution, because he's going to testify for the defense? Realization was starting to set in on him that maybe he had underestimated Oscar. Chewing on a piece of steak he had just placed in his mouth, he almost choked. He screamed, at no one, "that crooked butler Oscar, may be trying to blow everything for me. I won't let him; I won't let him no matter what it takes! If Oscar decides to side with them, he better watch his back because he will end up just like all the others who tried to cross me!"

Right at that very moment Geneva walked into the library. "Uncle Teddy, why are you so loud and who are you screaming at? And why are you in here sitting at grandfather's desk? I thought you said no one was to come in here until everything was settled." Teddy was already assuming the role of his father. He said he was sorry and he wasn't aware that he was loud. Then he said "what did you hear?"

"Oh, I didn't, I really couldn't understand what you were saying because you were loud and sounded so angry. Who or what has gotten under your skin?" Before he could answer, she said "you know it is only the two of us now. We have to trust and depend on each other, right, Uncle Teddy?"

Thinking before he answered her, he tried to read her facial expression, searching to see if she had heard anything and if she was really telling him the truth. Not really knowing who he could trust, Teddy knew he had to be at the top of the game or things would start landing on him. He wanted to change the conversation and focus it on what has been going on with her without arousing her suspicions, so he asked Geneva if she was still having those dreams. "Geneva, you haven't said anything about your dreams lately, did they just stop? Did you finally find out why they were saying my name? I know it wasn't anything worthwhile. You know that you can talk to me about anything and I will always be here for you."

Geneva said everything was alright. "I haven't seen much of you uncle since Friday night dinner. What have you been doing? Then Geneva said, "I guess we've just been too busy, passing each other by."

Teddy said "I guess so; I have been very busy trying to make sure everything continues to run as smoothly around here as possible." After that Teddy went back to eating his dinner, telling Geneva to make sure she ate some, because the cook had really made a very tasty meal for them. Then without even looking up while putting a spoon up to his mouth, Teddy said that he would talk to Geneva about everything later. So Geneva left her uncle in the library.

Geneva did go and eat her dinner, and while doing so, she began asking the cook a few questions and told him that her uncle was kind of upset. "Did anyone come by to see Uncle Teddy today?" He said no, but he thought maybe Oscar leaving without him knowing about it might have upset Mr. Teddy. Acting like she wasn't curious about Oscar, Geneva changed the subject. "Your steak has never been so tender and delicious, did you do something different this time?"

Blushing, he said" I'm glad that you like it; I really don't think I changed anything. But I might have-- I have been looking at a lot of different recipes lately." Then Geneva said as she was finishing up, (she hasn't been eating much during this whole ordeal) I sure hope you remember what you did to this steak. I could eat it every day."

When she arrived to the visiting room, there was Mr. Straitway, and he looked like he was smiling just a tiny bit. You see, Mr. Straitway hardly ever shows any emotions. Odessa walked over to the table where he was. After they greeted each other, he asked her to take a seat because they had a lot to discuss. Once she sat down he said "let's start from the beginning." He told Odessa that what they were about to talk about didn't go any farther, because if it did so it could hurt their case. She agreed to keep it between the two of them. Mr. Straitway asked Odessa so many questions, and showed her so many things that she was more confused than ever. She asked "Mr. Straitway, where does all of this leave me, and will it help our case?" He said "if we play our hand well it will not only help you, but we might be able to catch who ever set you up. How's does that sound to you?" Smiling at him, Odessa said "I believe I can live with that, and I will not say anything to anyone." Mr. Straitway said "very well, now I can get back to work on this before court on tomorrow. It's already late and I still haven't had my dinner yet. Mae Helen isn't going to like this-- this is the second time this week that I've been late or missed dinner altogether.

Odessa was happy but very tired when she got back to her cell. She laid down and whispered a short prayer before falling to sleep.

CHAPTER

17

IT'S MONDAY MORNING AND Mr. Straitway has gotten up early again; checking and double checking to make sure that he doesn't miss or leave anything. While eating his breakfast, he remembers something Odessa said to him last night. As he continued thinking about it, he thought "that will be a good question for Teddy and Mr. Johns both." He stopped eating for a moment to jot it down on a piece paper so that he wouldn't forget. "Which one them will lie about it first? That will then cause the other one to eventually have to tell the real truth, to try and save himself. I wonder which one will talk first?" Then Mr. Straitway laughed a little to himself while thinking, don't put the cart before the horse, and please don't let me count any of those chickens before they have hatched-- well not before they start talking. I wonder who Mr. Prod will be calling today; he had such a long list of witnesses I can't imagine who it will be. Just then Mae Helen asked, "Barry have you prayed this morning concerning which direction you should take? Then did you thank God for giving you His wisdom and understanding today? Barry, take that smirk off your face while I'm talking to you."

"I hear you dear; Mae Helen I have already done all that and more. I even fixed you and myself breakfast. Now will you please sit down here with me for just a few minutes, seeing it's almost time for me to leave?"

Mae Helen fixed her plate and gave him a kiss on the forehead before sitting down. "Thank you honey, this all looks so good I don't know what to taste first. I must have really been tired because I didn't even feel you getting out of the bed."

Barry said "that's good because I have been up since four thirty, and it was too early for you. I tried to make sure not to disturb you; I guess I did good, huh?"

"Yes, I guess you did, seeing you got in so late last night, but you are forgiven."

"Thanks dear, I have to be going. I will see you later."

"Okay, do well and be patient with yourself, and don't bite your nails either." Barry laughed as he went out the door.

Teddy is wide awake, wondering about his conversation with Geneva. "Has she remembered something and is just not telling me? Awe, Geneva wouldn't do that-- she trusts me, and like she said last night, we have to stick together."

Geneva has already left out early. She wants to try to see the judge before court starts. She wants to confess to helping in the murder of her beloved grandfather. She also wanted to tell Judge Watts about her parents' death, and that she was sure her Uncle Teddy was in on it as well. Geneva had to somehow convince the judge that she really didn't want to do it, and that she knows that her Uncle Teddy set her and Odessa both up. She was very scared of finding out what would become of her, yet she willing to take whatever punishment she had coming. Geneva felt it was only right to tell the truth.

Once Judge Watts heard everything Geneva had to say, he told her not to say anything about their meeting. Then Judge Watts said that he wanted to check out some things. He told Geneva that he would take care of this whole matter, and he sent her out the back way so no one would be the wiser about anything. The judge began to think about his dream; "maybe this is what I have been seeing." As he started to put on his robe, he whispered to himself, "God if you want or need my help, I'm here for you."

Walking into the courtroom, he saw that it was out of control. Teddy arrived in the courtroom, but was not able to locate Geneva. Teddy started thinking to himself "Pierre said Geneva had her breakfast and then she left out very early. I wonder why Geneva didn't wait for me? Where could Geneva have gone so early and why didn't she tell me last night of her plans?"

As soon as Teddy finished that thought, Mr. Johns tapped him on the shoulder. "Hey Teddy why haven't I heard from you? Is everything going as planned? You did take care of all those loose ends? Before Teddy could respond, Geneva walked up and gave him a big hug, and said how sorry she was that she couldn't wait for him. Teddy was so confused he didn't know who to answer first, or how he should respond to either of them. As he was about to open his mouth and address one of them, the sheriff announced court was about to start and "if you are a witness or have anything to do with this trial you need to go inside and take your seats quickly and quietly."

As they entered the courtroom, Judge Watts was taking his seat on the bench. He said "this court will come to order (as he was hitting his gavel on his desk). Bailiff, please close those doors and make sure everyone is seated and quiet in here. It is past time for this trial to get started and you know I don't like to be late."

"Is the prosecution ready to call their first witness for today?"

"Yes, we are your Honor. We will call Mr. Pierre Carbenos." Once he was on the stand and all sworn in, Mr. Prod started his questioning session. "So Mr. Carbenos, how long were you employed by the deceased? What was your job?"

He answered that he had been employed with the Osbournes since 1969. "I was hired to be the cook for the family as well as the entire staff, three meals a day, except on my off days or when I go on vacation, and that isn't very often."

"And how long have you known the defendant? And what can you tell this court about her?" (As he was pointing in the direction where Odessa was seated)

"Odessa has been with us about ***five** years now. She always goes home on the weekends, and returns very late on Sunday nights."

"How do you know that?"

"Because she enters in through the servants entrance, which is right below my quarters."

"So if that's all you know about her, why are you here today as a witness for the prosecution?"

"I'm here because I observed her a couple of days before Mr. Osbourne's death, taking a small valve from her pocket and putting it in Mr. Osbourne's tea. When I asked her what she was doing she became very nervous. And left the kitchen in a frightful hurry."

Mr. Prod picked up the bottle that they already have in evidence and showed it to the witness. "Did it look kind of like this bottle?"

"Yes, yes sir it looked exactly like that, that's the one she had that day when I saw her."

"Are you sure about this?"

"Oh yes, I would stake my life on it."

"Your Honor, the prosecution wants it noted that this witness has positively identified the bottle of poison that was found in the defendant's 1988 Ford Explorer, inside the trunk and inside the spare tire rim. Your Honor, I have no more questions for this witness."

Then the judge said "Mr. Straitway, your cross."

As he was approaching the witness stand, he stopped. "Your Honor, I have no questions for this witness at this time, but the defense reserves the right to call him at a later date during this trial."

Then Judge Watts said "the witness may step down and be called at a later time by the defense. Mr. Prod please call your next witness."

"Your Honor, the prosecution rests."

"Well I believe we can take an hour recess so the defense team can prepare to call their first witness in this trial. Mr. Straitway, you will be ready in an hour, yes?"

"Yes your Honor, the defense will be ready."

Then speaking to everyone in the courtroom, the judge said "this court will adjourned for one hour, and at such time we will come back here and proceed with this trial. (Then he stuck his table with his gavel) This court is adjourned. Then Judge Watts got up from the bench to leave the courtroom, and the bailiff asked everyone to rise as the judge left.

There in the hallway stood Markus Johns, impatiently waiting for Teddy to exit the courtroom. He wanted to get his questions answered from this morning, before Geneva had interrupted them, but there Teddy was with Geneva coming out of the courtroom. Mr. Johns waived to Teddy to come over, but Geneva was hugging and holding on to him as he was going over to talk to Mr. Johns. Now how in the world was he supposed to get answers with Geneva around? Mr. Johns spoke to them both, and then asked Geneva would she please excuse them for a few moments? "We have some pressing business that we need to discuss and we don't want to bore you with it." But Geneva protested and started pulling on Teddy as if she was two: "Uncle Teddy you promised me. You said that we would go across the street and have some of their famous burgers for lunch. Come on and hurry before the lines get too long and then we have to just get something from the vending machines." Mr. Johns suggested to Geneva that she should go on ahead. "Your Uncle Teddy and I will catch up with you. You will probably just be getting waited on when we get there." Geneva protested once again, pulled on her uncle, saying "what if you get there after I order? How will I pay for it? Come on Uncle Teddy, you promised." Mr. Johns was trying not to show how mad he was getting, so he took out his wallet and began shoving money in Geneva's hand. She wouldn't take it and let it fall to the floor. When he bent over to pick it up, she pulled her uncle out of there and across the street.

Teddy didn't know why, but he was kind of glad that Geneva was acting that way. He really didn't want to talk to Mr. Johns, seeing that he really didn't have any good news. During lunch, Teddy asked Geneva why she didn't wait for him this morning. "Where did you run off to? I'm sure I could have taken you wherever you wanted to go."

Geneva told him that after he asked her about the dreams she just felt like going and talking to them. "Uncle Teddy, I know you don't like going to the graveyard so I opted to go alone." That was only half of where she had gone, but she wasn't about to tell her uncle that she had a meeting with Judge Watts. Teddy tried to console her, as she looked as if she was going to just break down and cry. He told Geneva that he would do anything for her even if it meant going to the graveyard. That made Geneva laugh. "Uncle Teddy I know that, but I don't think that it would be necessary to put you through that kind of pain."

Teddy said, in a macho voice, "what pain?"

Geneva laughed and said "the kind that I saw on your face when I told you where I was this morning." They both laughed, and then Teddy said "you have got a valid point there my little sweet pea."

"Why Uncle Teddy, you haven't called me that in a very long time. Thanks for bringing me here; I enjoyed spending this time with you."

"Wait-- who brought who here?"

Geneva said "I guess we brought each other here" and they started to laugh again. Then Teddy, looking down at his watch, said "we better get going before the courtroom fills up."

Back at court, in a far corner, Mr. Johns was talking to a couple of real shady looking characters. They were asking Mr. Johns a lot of questions and he was answering them as best as he could. Then Mr. Johns looked up and saw Teddy and Geneva, and he called out to Teddy "come over and meet the people I was telling you about earlier." But Geneva was pulling Teddy right into the courtroom, saying "we have to get seats before there aren't any more left. And if you all are planning to come in, you better hurry before you end up standing right where you are until everything is over." Teddy could see Mr. Johns' face was turning red as they entered the courtroom. Again, Teddy was happy about the way Geneva was acting today may just have saved him from something really bad happening.

Mr. Johns came in just as the sheriffs were closing the doors and saying "there are only a few seats left, and once they are gone you have to remain out here in the hallway very quietly while the court is in session." Teddy could see Mr. Johns was looking around for him, so he began looking in another direction so there would be no eye contact between them.

Once he spotted Teddy, Mr. Johns took his seat. He thought to himself "Teddy doesn't know who he's messing with. These people that I'm in bed with want answers and they know how to exact those answers. Teddy better be very careful; it would be better to talk to me than it would be talking to them. He better stop avoiding me or he will end up like the rest of his family. Then we will just deal with that bratty niece of his. Geneva won't be a problem."

The bailiff asked everyone in the courtroom to stand. "This court is now in session, and the Honorable Judge Watts is presiding over this case, the state of Illinois verses Odessa Princeton. This is a murder trial and we ask that everyone remain seated and quiet. Please if you hear your name called, please get up and come down to the front as swiftly as you can. This court thanks you for your indulgence and your patience."

"Mr. Straitway are you ready to call your first witness?"

"Yes, your Honor, the defense would like to call Dr. Oliver Johnston to the stand." Once the bailiff swore the doctor in, Judge Watts said "Mr. Straitway you can now examine your first witness."

"Now Dr. Johnston, please tell this court how you knew the deceased?"

"I have been his physician for over thirty five years."

"When was the last time you saw the deceased alive?"

"I saw him on that Monday before he died."

"Was there anything that concerned you about his health?"

"Yes, Mr. Osbourne had a cold for far too long and he had been coughing a lot. I had drawn some of his blood to have the lab run a few tests and cultures on him. I spoke to Odessa privately, I told her of my concerns. I asked her to call me if there were any changes with that cold, I feared it could easily turn into pneumonia. I then asked Odessa to watch over Mr. Osbourne closely, especially if the coughing got worse. Odessa was concerned as well, and promised to call me with any changes. That's what she did the day he died."

"Do you feel Odessa reacted in a timely manner?"

"Yes, I believe she called me as soon as she saw he was in trouble. Odessa would never have allowed Mr. Osbourne to suffer knowingly."

"What do you feel happened to the deceased?"

"He was poisoned."

"Doctor, you said that like you were sure, how do you know that?"

"The cultures and the other blood tests that I took and sent to the lab came back positive for it."

"How long have you known this?"

"The results came back the day of his death. That's where I was when Odessa called me concerning his health."

"Your Honor I have no more questions for this witness."

"Your cross, Mr. Prod."

Mr. Prod began to question the doctor. "Did you see the deceased the day in question, at any time before he was murdered?"

"No, I didn't."

"You stated that he was still coughing, as per the message left by the defendant. So doctor you don't really know for sure if the deceased was still coughing or having problems breathing. For all you know, Mr. Osbourne could've already been dead."

"Objection, Your Honor."

"On what grounds counsellor?"

"Hearsay and leading the witness."

"Those last two questions will be stricken from the court records, and the jury will disregard those last remarks from the prosecutor. Mr. Prod I am warning you to be careful. You may continue."

"Did you know that Mr. Osbourne was sick and that he had a really bad cough that day? Would you say it was a crime of passion?"

"Objection, Your Honor."

"On what grounds?"

"Leading the witness."

"The doctor wasn't there so how would he know what happened? Did the deceased ever tell you that the defendant," pointing at Odessa "was forcing her beliefs on him?"

"No, he never did."

"Are you sure, or did you really take your patient's whole well-being into consideration?"

"Mr. Osbourne never expressed that to me. He loved and trusted Odessa."

"Mr. Prod shouted, "and look where that trust got him! If you had just called the authorities, maybe the deceased would still be alive!"

"Objection, Your Honor. Mr. Prod is beating up on this witness."

"You said he trusted her with information in his will, and when he made changes to it, she killed him didn't she!"

"I didn't say that. I know Odessa wouldn't have done anything to harm Mr. Osbourne."

"Were you there? What about (holding up the prosecution exhibit #3) these patches? Do you know where they came from?"

"I'm sure I don't know; I have never seen them before."

"Well Doctor, this is what the coroner is saying that caused his death. The defendant used this to administer poison to the deceased on a daily basis. Now do you still say that the defendant wouldn't harm anyone, such as Mr. Osbourne? She murdered him didn't she?"

"I still don't-- and can't-- believe Odessa had anything to do with his death, no matter what you show me. Odessa's message was clear as day, she was genuinely worried about him. Odessa wanted me to hurry up and get there to see about Mr. Osbourne. Her phone call to me was a cry for help, not one of someone committing murder. Odessa is a good nurse and I say she was truly his friend."

"Friends you say, huh? With friends like her, who needs enemies? Or did she just call you because she suddenly remembered her trespasses at that moment? Then fearing she may get caught, she called you to give herself a strong and much needed alibi."

"Objection, Your Honor."

Judge Watts, addressing the prosecutor, said "Mr. Prod, watch yourself and tread very lightly. I'm warning you for my last time today! You may continue."

"I have no more questions for this witness."

The Judge asked Mr. Straitway, "Redirect?"

"Yes, your Honor. I have two more question for this witness. Doctor in your own words, and from what you have observed of the two of them together, do you feel that Odessa is capable of murdering anyone? And do you feel she murdered her friend Mr. Osbourne?"

"No. I do not believe she could murder anyone; never in a million years. Odessa couldn't hurt a fly. She loved Mr. Osbourne, they were friends."

"Your Honor, I'm finished with this witness."

Judge Watts then said "due to the lateness of the hour; this court will reconvene tomorrow morning at 10 a.m. sharp. (Hitting his gavel on the table) You are all dismissed." Then the bailiff asked everyone to stand as Judge Watts was leaving the courtroom, and please exit the courtroom and building in an orderly fashion.

Mr. Johns was outside again waiting to talk to Teddy. As soon as Geneva got into the car, one of his associates placed his arm under Teddy's arm and they walked him over toward Mr. Johns, who was looking very angry. "Teddy did you just think you could avoid me all day? Now were you successful in tying up all your loose ends?"

"Yeah," Teddy said very nervously."

"So we won't have any surprises, will we Teddy, or you will get the surprise of your life. Do we have an understanding, Teddy?"

"Yes, yes, you know I don't want any trouble."

All this time Geneva was looking out at them, and wondering who those two men were. She watched the one lead her uncle away from the car, but why? What were they talking about? And why did Mr. Johns let them, or have them, grab her uncle? What was that all about? Maybe she would ask her uncle when he came back to the car.

Odessa had been lying down ever since they brought her back from court. Now it's dinner time at the jail and she is not only tired but she's very hungry. She doesn't ever remember being excited about mealtime here, ever. But it's different this evening-- Odessa feels like she hadn't ate in months. When guard placed her tray in the window, she grabbed the biscuit off the tray so fast and stuffed it into her mouth without thinking. The guard said "my, my, somebody's ready to eat." Odessa, feeling a little embarrassed, took part of the biscuit out of her mouth that she hadn't already eaten. Wiping her mouth, she smiled and said yes. He went on helping to deliver the trays to the other inmates. Odessa stopped and prayed over her food and thanked God for it, and prayed for all those that were less fortunate than herself. After eating her dinner, her plan was to read some from her Bible and get some rest before the trial tomorrow.

Teddy has been busy since he returned home today from court. He was tired and very scared. Mr. Johns has been calling him since he got there, asking him all kinds of questions-- more than he had previously asked-- and giving him ultimatums. Pierre brought Teddy his dinner but Teddy is so upset he can't even think about eating.

Besides, after those phone calls he has lost his appetite and hasn't gone near his plate, not even for a whiff of it.

Mae Helen has prepared a fine meal for their dinner. Barry is already sitting down at the table waiting for his plate. As she handed Barry his plate, Mae Helen asked how he felt the trial went today. "Alright I think, the prosecution rested and I had the chance to call my first witness to the stand."

"Who did you finally decide to call first?"

"I decided to have the deceased man's doctor as my first witness. Prod tried to cross him up, but I feel the doctor handled himself very well."

"Wow, I can't wait to see what Darwine has to say about the trial. He will be coming on in about twenty minutes, and I have to finish the dishes so I don't miss him."

"Don't worry about that, I'll help you with the dishes and we will both watch Darwine."

Mae Helen said "you're so sweet and thoughtful, that's one of the reasons why I married you." Blushing, Barry started to remove the dishes and take them into the kitchen.

"Good evening everyone, and welcome back to all those that watch each weeknight. I am Darwine Trestor, your anchor here at WNT. Look who's back: our lovely co-anchor Ms. Veronica Best. Doesn't she look pretty and well rested? (Applauding in the station) Veronica, you know that everyone has missed you, and some even felt you left because you were having a bit of a breakdown. (Laughing in the studio) They called into the station, just like they did that day we pulled that stunt. They were all wondering if you were coming back. Well, here she is in the flesh; your eyes are not playing tricks on you. (Laughing and applauding in the studio) Again our very own co- anchor Ms. Veronica Best. (More applauding in the studio) Okay I know you're waiting for the updates from today's trial.

"Prosecutor Prod called his last witness of this trial today. The deceased's cook, Pierre something. Wow, Mr. Prod had some kind of line up; I hate to see them come to an end. I Wonder if the defense also has a bountiful list of witnesses? Now as for the prosecution's last witnesses: I hope Pierre has been saving up some of his money. I hope he already has some job offers lined up. Definitely, after your last employer died from being poisoned, I think it would be very hard to find employment, especially another job as a cook anywhere. Did I hear him say that he was still on staff at the Osbourne's mansion? I don't think I would eat his food, do you? (Laughing in the studio) Somebody poisoned that poor Mr. Osbourne. The cook says that he saw the defendant putting something in the deceased's tea, and he identified the prosecution's Exhibit #3 as the bottle that he said the defendant had a couple days before the deceased died. But you can rest assure that the defense attorney Mr. Straitway didn't let them get away with it. Once again he came out swinging, he was throwing objections out at all of it. Did you see Judge Watts was ruling all in his favor? One would think that they were friends. Maybe Mr. Prod better watch out if they are, seeing that there are a lot of strange friendships going around this trial.

"After lunch the defense called for their first witness, the deceased's doctor, Doctor Johnston to the stand for questioning. He had been the deceased man's doctor for thirty five years. The doctor said that his patient had a bad cough for some time. He and the defendant were both very concerned about it. He also said he had drawn blood from the deceased to have some lab work done. He said when the results came back that Mr. Osbourne had truly been poisoned. That proves he was really murdered-- so who is the real murderer in this case? He also stated under oath that the defendant didn't do it. So who did this? Does anyone have a clue as who wanted the deceased dead?

"Did everyone see how Mr. Prod went straight for the doctor's jugular? Take notes Mr. Straitway, that's the way you do it. Mr. Prod kept hamming those questions at him about the defendant. He is set on destroying her credibility and accusing her of this murder. But the doctor wasn't shaken by Mr. Prod-- he stood his ground, I think, don't you? Mr. Prod couldn't break him, but check out how Mr. Straitway came back on his redirect. (Applauding at the station) The doctor said the defendant couldn't hurt a fly. Do you think that the doctor is just covering up for her by saying that they were friends.

He went on to say that the defendant loved the deceased. How? (Lots of laughing) Did you see how fast Judge Watts looked away when he said that? As soon as the witnesses stepped down, the judge was ready to go. I know he was thinking the same thing just like us. (More laughter) Well, we will just have to wait for that piece of information to come out, if it ever does. Maybe it will later on down the road, after this trial.

"This is anchor Darwine Trestor, and co-anchor Veronica Best saying good night, from everyone at WNT, Worldly News Tonight. We are glad that you all tuned in to watch us each evening. We look forward to giving you more updates from this exciting trial. Tune in tomorrow evening at this same time. Again have a good and safe night."

CHAPTER 18

It's Tuesday morning and the trial is already in full gear. The defense has called Mr. Markus Johns to the stand, to be treated as a hostile witness. "Mr. Johns, please tell this court what you and Mr. Theodore Osbourne were shouting about so early in morning, the very same day of your client's death?"

"I don't know what you are talking about?"

"What was so urgent that you had to get there before the chickens got up?"

"Again, I say I don't know what you are talking about, or where you are getting your information from, but I'm sorry sir your informants are wrong and they got nothing on me."

"When was the last time you spoke to Mr. Osbourne, the deceased?"

"I spoke to him the night before his death."

"Please tell this court what his last words to you were?"

"That is attorney and client privileged information, but if you must know it was about changes he wanted made to his will."

"Are you sure about the wills?"

"I didn't say wills, I said will, meaning one, and you do know how to count."

"Did you ever make more than one will at a time for the deceased to sign?"

"Why would I do something like that? that is unethical."

"Have you told this court everything you know about Mr. Osbourne's death?"

"How would I know anything to tell you about his death? Shouldn't you be asking your client that question, I believe she's the one on trial for his murder."

"Did you, or anyone you know, take part of the murder plot to kill Rebecca Osbourne-Trice?"

"What are you talking about? Everyone knows her death was proven to be an accident." Mr. Johns pulled out his handkerchief and started to wipe his forehead, as he was sweating badly. Then he continued, "again I tell you that you need to get yourself a better group of informants or investigators, because the ones you have now, they need to find themselves a new line of work."

"What do you really know about Mr. Harrington Osbourne, III's death?"

"I've told you I wasn't there, ask your client."

"Objection, Your Honor."

"On what grounds Mr. Prod?"

"Harassment. The question has been asked and answered already by the witness."

"Objection sustained. Those last questions and answers will be stricken from these court proceedings, and the jury will disregard that last question from the defense attorney and as well the last answer from the witness. Mr. Straitway watch your steps. Do you have any more questions for this witness?"

"No, Your Honor."

"Mr. Prod redirect?"

"Mr. Johns, where were you when the deceased died?"

"In my office, preparing Mr. Osbourne's will as he asked me to do. He wanted it Friday, which was the very next day."

"Your Honor I have no more questions for this witness."

"The witness may step down. Mr. Straitway you can call your next witness after this court takes a thirty minute break."

The Judge called for a thirty minute break after Mr. Johns' testimony. Judge Watts asked that all witnesses remain in the courtroom during the short break. Once everyone else was out of the courtroom, the witnesses were all lead to a room with a very long table with chairs all around it. They were asked not to talk among themselves. Teddy was very nervous and tried to leave, but the sheriff asked him to please have a seat. The sheriff informed them that they would be bringing each of them a snack and something to drink shortly.

During the break, they used a search warrant to search Mr. Johns' office. They found all kinds of documents that showed that he and his associates were going to do a hostile takeover of Teddy's family business. Notes concerning the poison and the real receipt for it were also there. There was a jar hidden in his office; it was half full of the same poison that was found in the deceased body.

When the break was over, Mr. Straitway called yet another hostile witness to the stand, Mr. Theodore Osbourne. "Mr. Osbourne, tell us in your own words what you and Mr. Johns were arguing about on the morning that your father died? Oh, please forgive me, you have been crying 'murder' from the second he stopped breathing. Am I correct about this?"

"I don't know what you are talking about."

"Didn't Mr. Johns call you that Wednesday night after he talked to your father?"

"He may have, I don't recall."

"You don't recall which part: the part that he called you or that you two were arguing early the morning of your father's death?"

"I said I don't know. I don't know what you are talking about."

"So when Mr. Johns and you were talking that morning, he told you that you better do something, didn't he?"

"I, I…" Teddy was getting very nervous on the stand. When Mr. Straitway saw that, he knew he was on the right track. So he continued with his line of questioning. "How did you know that your father had been murdered?" Before Teddy could answer, Mr. Straitway kept talking at him, seeing Teddy was about to break. "The paramedics had just stopped performing CPR on him, and hadn't even pronounced him dead yet. But you came hurrying into the library with policemen in tow at that precise moment. Do you have E.S.P? Who called them? Why were they called? When did you call them, for them to get to the mansion so fast? Do you have them on speed dial, and I mean speed." Teddy started shouting "it was all Mr. Johns, he planned it all. He told me that my father was changing his will, and that I would be totally cut out. He told me to take care of it. He said it was for the good of the business. Mr. Johns planned it all, I tell you."

Mr. Johns jumped up from his seat in the back of the court room and started screaming. "That's an outright lie. I didn't tell Teddy to do anything. Teddy you better watch what you're saying!"

The courtroom was in an uproar, with everyone talking and the reporters taking great notes and pictures for the evening news. Judge Watts pounded his gavel on the table, calling for order in his courtroom. "I will not tolerate outbursts like that in my courtroom. Sheriff, sit those people down in the back, this court will come to order! Or I will have every last one of you found in contempt of this court! Have I made myself clear, does everyone in here understand?"

Meanwhile, Mr. Prod was very angry with his team because he doesn't like surprises. How in the world does the defense know about this? Mr. Prod told his team they better get him some information on these new developments. The courtroom had calmed down, and Judge Watts asked Mr. Straitway if he had any more questions for this witness. He said "no, Your Honor."

"Redirect Mr. Prod?"

"No, Your Honor."

The judge said "the witness may step down." As Teddy was going back to his seat, the judge asked Mr. Straitway to call his next witness.

Next the defense called Oscar to the stand. Right after the bailiff swore him in, Mr. Straitway jumped right in with his questions. "Where are you employed, and what is your job description?"

"I recently resigned from my job as butler at the Osbourne mansion."

"Who hired you for that job?"

"Mr. Osbourne himself."

"How well did you know the deceased?"

"I was his personal butler and friend."

"Have you ever met the defendant?"

"Yes I know her; she was Mr. Osbourne's nurse."

"How well would you say you know her?"

"I feel I know her pretty well."

"Do you feel that she is capable of murder?"

"Objection Your Honor, goes to speculation." Prod interjected.

"Overruled. I think this court wants to hear what he has to say."

"No she isn't, and besides, she's not wired like that." Oscar continued.

"Why do you say that?"

"Because she is kind to everyone, and she and 'Mr. O' as she fondly called him, were friends."

"Objection, Your Honor, speculation."

"I'll allow it, this time" the Judge ruled.

"How well, and what do you know about, the deceased's son?"

"Pretty well I would say, but he and I haven't seen eye to eye on a lot of things over the years."

"Why is that?"

"Because Teddy wants to do what he wants to do, and I did only what his father told me to do."

"How did he and his father get along?"

"They didn't. Mr. Teddy was always coming up with different schemes to make more money. And he would try and get his father to buy into it. He wanted Mr. O to turn the business over to him. Mr. Osbourne always said 'I don't know why Teddy just can't wait until I'm dead?' But Teddy couldn't and didn't want to wait, because he was always spending too much money, more than he made. His father said Teddy would just run the company into the ground in under a year, and there would be no inheritance for his granddaughter Geneva. Mr. Osbourne loved Geneva so much he was leaving her the Osbourne mansion and the majority of the company's stock, which he owned, not to mention the various other things that he had chosen to leave Geneva in his will. Mr. Osbourne also was leaving Odessa a substantial amount, and some for her church, as he really liked her pastor. Mr. Osbourne left me a decent amount as well. We were friends, you know. I was Mr. Osbourne's trusted butler for over twenty three years. He trusted me with a lot of things, and he really loved his staff."

"You said he trusted you with a lot of things, such as… ? Do you know anything about the deceased's death?"

"Yes, he was poisoned."

"How do you know this, other than it has been mentioned several times doing this trial?"

"Because Mr. Osbourne told me so."

"Do you have any other information about the deceased that would prove this?"

"Yes I have those tapes and pictures over there on your table."

"Your Honor, the defense would like these pictures and tapes placed into evidence for the defense, as Exhibit #1 and #2." Judge Watts said "so noted, they will now be known as Exhibits #1 and #2 for the duration of this trial."

Teddy and Mr. Johns both tried to sneak out of the courtroom while Oscar is on the stand, but the judge had already told the sheriffs not to allow anyone to leave before he dismissed everyone.

"Oscar please tell this court, how did you come by all of this?"

"I got them out of Mr. Osbourne's safe. Mr. Osbourne gave me the combination to it after he changed the old combination."

"Why did the deceased give you the new combination, and why did he give it only to you?"

"I was his friend and I was the only one with the new combination to the safe that he wanted to have it. He gave it to me so I could put the tapes and other things in it."

Prod had heard enough. "Objection! Objection, Your Honor."

"On what grounds, Mr. Prod?"

"Hearsay. All of it is just hearsay."

"Overruled. I will allow it. I feel that it may be relevant to this case." Mr. Prod didn't like that, as he felt that he may be losing ground with the jury.

"Where did you get the tapes that you placed in the safe for the deceased?"

"From the hidden camera in the kitchen that was located on top of the cabinets."

"How often were you told to remove the tapes and place them into the deceased's safe, and how long have you been doing it?"

"I was told to remove and replace each tape daily. I have been doing this for about three months."

"When was the last time you changed the tape?"

"The night that Mr. Osbourne died, that was the last time he asked me to do it."

"Who put that camera there and for what reason?"

"Mr. Osbourne had me to place it there out of sight so that he could confirm his suspicions."

"What kind of suspicions did the deceased have?"

"He knew Mr. Teddy was angry with him, and he was having a lot of strange symptoms in his body, so he put two and two together."

"What else did he do?"

"He started changing his will more and more to see what Mr. Teddy and others that were involved would do. Mr. Osbourne wanted to make them show their hands."

"What happened after that?"

Oscar began to cry, "just what he suspected, they murdered my employer and friend. I asked him to stop, but when he saw the tapes he wanted to protect his only granddaughter Geneva from the one that he felt had murdered her parents."

"What are you saying?"

"That Wednesday after Mr. Osbourne retired for the evening, he received a very important phone call. That call gave him the proof that his beloved Rebecca and her husband weren't just in an accident but that they had been murdered. Then Mr. Osbourne called and informed Mr. Johns of some of what he had just learned, and told Mr. Johns that he wanted some changes to his will done right away. Mr. Osbourne wanted them all done and in his hand by Friday morning."

"What happened after that?"

"Mr. Osbourne called me to his room and told me all that I have told you. I wish they would have just left Mr. Osbourne alone-- he was already dying. Mr. Osbourne would have died in a couple months anyway. He had bone cancer; he didn't want anyone to know it."

"Then how did you find out?"

"He and Dr. Johnston told me. That's why I would give Pierre his menu each day."

"You mean his nurse, the defendant, and friend wasn't aware of this?"

Before Oscar could answer the question, he looked over at Odessa, who was crying. He said "I'm sorry, he didn't want you to know. Mr. Osbourne knew if you knew, that Teddy and others may find out. He knew you loved him and that you might have let on about it without being aware of it."

"Objection, this is hogwash. Where is the proof of this secret illness? Does the defense have any concrete evidence to support these allegations?"

"Yes we do, Your Honor. We have sworn affidavits to support this witness testimony. And the defense would like to offer them into evidence at this time as Exhibits #3 and #4."

"So noted. This evidence will become part of this court and trial proceedings. Objection overruled. Please continue, Mr. Straitway, with this witness."

"Why didn't Mr. Osbourne tell his only son Teddy about his illness?"

"Mr. Osbourne felt that Teddy may have taken him to court for an incompetence hearing, stating that Mr. Osbourne wasn't able to handle his daily business affairs. Then Mr. Teddy would take the business away from him by default. Mr. Osbourne didn't want that to happen, and that's why he had to do what he did. Mr. Osbourne knew there was no other way, but to sacrifice himself for all those that he loved and that he would be leaving behind." Wiping the tears from his eyes, Oscar said "he was a great man and he was my friend. You all didn't have to do him like that, Mr. Teddy he loved you in spite of your faults and he prayed every night for you."

Mr. Straitway said "Your Honor, I have no more questions for this witness." As Mr. Straitway went to take his seat, Judge Watts looked over in Mr. Prod's direction and said "your cross, Mr. Prod."

"I don't have any at this time, Your Honor." Then Judge Watts said "the witness may step down and take his seat."

Mr. Johns and Teddy were still trying desperately to leave the courtroom. Judge Watts ordered the sheriffs to detain Mr. Theodore

Osbourne and Mr. Markus Johns, and hold them over for questioning in the murder of Mr. Harrington Osbourne, III; and their arrests for murder, or maybe murders, depending on the outcome of this trial. Then the judge asked that Teddy and Mr. Johns be removed from his courtroom. Once they were removed, the judge said "after all today's twists and turns in this case, this court will reconvene on Thursday morning at nine o'clock sharp. When this court is back in session on Thursday, the defense will continue with their witnesses. This court is now adjourned."

Before leaving the courtroom, Odessa asked Mr. Straitway if he knew Oscar was going to say what he did today. "No, but I hoped that he wouldn't hold back. That is the only way that we can help get that jury to set you free."

Back in her cell, Odessa still didn't know what to think about everything that happened in court today. She was very saddened by what Oscar said from the witness box. She didn't have one clue that Mr. O was dying. "Why didn't he trust me? We had other secrets, and I never told anyone. I pray that he wasn't suffering and feeling that he couldn't tell me. I could've spent more time with him, I hope he knew that." Odessa was still crying. "Well I guess Mr. O knew what was best for us all."

Geneva was back at the mansion, lying across her bed, still in somewhat of a daze from all that was said and went down in the courtroom today. She has being crying, thinking about her grandfather and his unselfish love he extended to her and others. "I feel so bad for treating Odessa the way I did. She had nothing to do with all of this; it was Uncle Teddy and Mr. Johns all the time. I should've talked more to grandfather." She began crying even harder. "I hope they lock them both up and throw away the keys."

Mae Helen had heard and seen a short clip from the trial earlier in the evening. She could hardly wait for Barry to get home so she could question him about it. Mae Helen was finishing up their dinner when Barry arrived back at home. No sooner than Barry hung up his jacket, Mae Helen jumped right in with all sorts of questions for him. "Can you wait one minute honey; I need to catch my breath. It was a circus outside the courtroom today, all the media and reporters everywhere."

Mae Helen jumped right in. "Yes I saw you on T.V.; you looked so good. (And tired, she thought to herself) Barry what happened?"

"Mae Helen, I am tired and hungry, and if you feed me I will tell you any and everything you want to know."

Mae Helen started laughing. "I was just thinking that same thing," while placing his plate on the table in front of him.

"What's so funny, I want to laugh too?"

"It was nothing, eat your food and we will talk when you're finished like you said. You know I want to see what they have to say on WNT, they will be on in thirty minutes."

Right after dinner, Odessa was told she had a visitor waiting for her. She thought it would be her dad or Mr. Straitway who had come to visit her, but she never in a million years would have thought of this person. She tried not to look so shocked and surprised. When she walked over to the table, she got something else that was unexpected. Geneva jumped up and gave her a huge hug, while saying how sorry she was about everything that had happened. Odessa hugged her right back and told her "it's okay, we all make mistakes and come up short. That's why Jesus died for us all. He loves us in spite of ourselves."

Geneva asked "can you ever forgive me?"

Odessa said "I already have! I did it a long time ago, and I love you and there is nothing that you can do about it." They talked for an hour or so, it was very good and productive for both of them.

"Good evening, this is anchor Darwine Trestor and co-anchor Ms. Veronica Best, reporting on today's trial. We at WNT would like to say welcome to all our viewers out there. Veronica, you were in the courtroom today. I bet you couldn't believe your eyes and ears."

"Well, Darwine, it started off like a firecracker and ended up with a big bang. I'll let you tell our audience what happened today from the beginning, go for it Darwine."

"It all started when the defense called Mr. Markus Johns, the deceased's attorney, to the stand. Mr. Straitway asked the judge that

Mr. Johns be treated as a hostile witness. No sooner than attorney Straitway asked his first question, you could see the witness wasn't going to cooperate. Mr. Johns started out getting smart with Mr. Straitway, telling him about his informants, how they had nothing on him, and that Mr. Straitway needed to get new ones. Mr. Johns really didn't say what he and the deceased talked about, avoiding that question as if it were a plague. The tides turned when the defense asked him about the murder of the deceased's daughter, Rebecca Osbourne-Trice. By this time, Mr. Johns was sweating all over the place. His reply was that her death was ruled as an accident and everybody knows it, again saying he needed to find some new investigators and informants, and his current ones need to get into a different line of work.

"After that, the judge called for a thirty minute break, and he had all the witnesses stay in the courtroom. What was that all about?

Next the defense called yet another hostile witness to the stand, the deceased's son Mr. Teddy. Mr. Straitway asked Mr. Teddy about the conversation that he and Mr. Johns had on the morning of his father's death. Teddy said he didn't know what he was talking about. Then Mr. Straitway asked Teddy did he have the police on speed dial. I thought they lived in a very nice and quiet area. Especially with all that land around their mansion. Mr. Teddy must have gotten a little confused, and kind of nervous because out of nowhere he started blaming his family's attorney for everything, telling the entire courtroom that the attorney planned it all, from the wills to the murder.

"But wait, Mr. Markus Johns didn't like that. He was shouting from the back of the courtroom, calling Mr. Teddy a liar. Then he said that Teddy better watch what he was saying! Hey was that a threat? I don't know about you all, but I think it was. I know you all can't guess what happened next: the courtroom went up in an uproar. Cameras were flashing from all directions. Judge Watts didn't like it one bit and he said so, saying that he would have everyone placed in contempt of court.

"Now here comes the best part of this trial, for me. You have always heard them say that the butler did it, right? Wrong, that's not so for this one; he has the real data on everybody. And he brought his proof to court; he had tapes and pictures. What was so sad, was when he revealed to the defendant and everyone in the courtroom that the deceased, Mr. Harrington Osbourne, III was going to die on his own in just a couple of months. Did you see the defendant Odessa's face when he said that? Tears were running all down her cheeks. She really hadn't any idea that her friend and employer was dying, and not just from the poison. He said that they didn't have to murder him. He also told the court that after watching the tapes of them poisoning him every day, Mr. Osbourne decided to sacrifice himself. All he wanted to do was protect his granddaughter Geneva, and all of the others that he would be leaving behind. One of his biggest fears was that his son, Teddy would take his business away from him. The butler was crying when he said it, and that the deceased loved his son and that he always prayed for him every night without fail. Wow, I feel like if I had met the deceased, Mr. Osbourne, in person before his untimely death; that he would have really been a nice person to know and to have in your corner.

"Veronica you were there when they made those arrests."

"Yes I was. They arrested the deceased's son and his attorney. Now who will defend the son? He and Mr. Johns are both in the slammer. Did they plan this, or was there a plan at all? Now who will Mr. Teddy hire to get him off? I wonder how Mr. Teddy is doing tonight, after finding out today his father was already dying, and he allegedly helped to kill him.

"Prosecutor Prod was objecting, but it didn't matter because Mr. Straitway had done his homework. I don't think the prosecution saw any of this coming. They probably felt like they weren't even in the courtroom at all. Did you get a look at Mr. Prod when they had all those cameras on him? He looked as if he was letting his team have it again today. Mr. Prod looked puzzled as if he was lost., I have never seen Mr. Prod like that, have you? Mr. Prod better be careful and watch out-- this trial could be getting away from him. Call in and tell us how you feel about today's trial. This Is Darwine Trestor and co-anchor Ms. Veronica Best at WNT, Worldly News Tonight, saying goodnight to you all. We'll have more updates for you on Thursday evening. Again we say goodnight from all of us at WNT."

CHAPTER
19

GENEVA HAD SCHEDULED ANOTHER meeting with Judge Watts on Wednesday afternoon. One of her questions, among others, was whether or not she was going to be arrested as well. The judge told her there was nothing for her to fear, and that she hadn't harmed her grandfather. Once the meeting was over, Geneva left and went back to the mansion.

She had a lot to think about, and a lot of things to take care of on her own. She wondered about her Uncle Teddy, and how he was doing since his arrest yesterday. She still loved him and wanted to help him, but didn't have a clue as to how she would even go about it. Walking down the long hall of the mansion, she turned and without thinking she went inside the forbidden library. Uncle Teddy had said that it was off limits to everyone until the trial was over. Yet he was in there screaming his head off, about what he never explained, saying he would do it later. Still in deep thought, and not paying attention, she didn't know that Oscar was in there with her. When he spoke to her, she was very startled. "What are you doing here? I thought that you left. Didn't you say on the stand that you had resigned? How did you get back in here, who was it that let you in?"

Oscar started off by telling her he was sorry for everything that she was going through, but he had some unfinished business to attend to. "What is that?" she asked. He asked her to please close the door, and asked if he could talk to her about her grandfather. He told Geneva she can trust him to tell her everything, and that he had something for her to look at. Reluctantly she agreed. "I don't who I can trust, but go ahead say what you have to say, and show me whatever you have to."

Geneva was so upset and bewildered she just flopped down in a chair near the desk. Oscar first walked over to the screen and pulled it down, then he started the film. Geneva began crying. It was a message to her from her grandfather, explaining all that had gone on. Her grandfather made it the day of his death. He apologized for leaving her so soon, but it was the only way he could protect her. He asked her to take Oscar back into her employment and that he would help her with everything.

After she had calmed down, Oscar gave her a lot of legal documents from out of the safe. Then he walked over to the desk and pushed a button underneath it. From behind her, she heard the bookcase moving. Geneva turned around to see a very large room with all kinds of files in it. "What is all that she asked?"

"The Osbourne family business designs and plans, all of them since the conception. Now they all belong to you, it's your company Ms. Geneva." Geneva didn't know how to respond to that, but she did ask Oscar if would he stay on and help her with everything. Oscar said he would be delighted to do so. "I have been groomed for some time by your grandfather to help you. And it will be my pleasure to help, and watch the fourth generation of Osbournes go to the next level, with the ability to provide for and support all the charities and the community groups that Mr. Osbourne loved. Then Geneva gave Oscar a big hug and said "let's do it, and do it the way the Osbournes have done in the past, just bigger!" They both laughed. Then Oscar said "what would you like for dinner?"

It is Wednesday evening, and Mr. Johns and Mr. Teddy are still been questioned by the authorities. When Detective Rodgers told them that they were being charged with premeditated murder, Mr. Johns said he wanted his lawyer. Then Detective Rodgers reminded Teddy that his lawyer had been charged as well, so he would need to find a different one.

They gave both Mr. Johns and Teddy a chance to take a deal. The reward for the deal was that whichever one took it would avoid the death penalty and would instead face life imprisonment without parole. Teddy, being the weaker link, was scared and with the constant pressure of it all, didn't want Mr. Johns to beat him to it, so he said he'd take the deal.

They told Teddy the plea bargain would only be given to him in exchange for turning State's evidence against Mr. Johns. The State also stated they would only accept Teddy's plea if he told them everything about what happened in the deaths of Mr. Osbourne, his sister Rebecca and her husband, and also about Mr. Johns and his associates. They gave him the papers to sign and he did.

Teddy started out by telling them everything that was said the morning of his father's death, and what lead to all of it. "Mr. Johns called me that Wednesday night after he'd talked with my father. He told me that my father said that he had solid concrete evidence that Rebecca and her husband Freddrick were murdered. Then Mr. Johns asked me 'how could that be?' Before slamming his phone down in my ear, he told me to expect him at seven in the morning. That morning he arrived at a quarter to seven. We went into my office to talk, but he started shouting at the top of his lungs at me, ordering me to get the combination to the safe and find out what else is in it. Mr. Johns wanted to know what else my father knew, and what he was hiding from him. Mr. Johns told me that he wasn't playing around and that I'd better get this situation under control. Mr. Johns said he had done all that he could, and if I didn't finish what was started, I was going to be the fall guy. So where do you think that left me? He said I'd better do whatever it takes to finish the job, and put a final end to the whole stinking matter, or they would. Teddy continued talking to the detectives and the State way into the night.

Thursday morning has finally arrived, with everyone sitting on the edge of their seats waiting to see what's going to happen in court today. The court has been in session for twenty minutes now, and the defense has had them call Mr. Brice to the stand.

Mr. Straitway's first question to Mr. Brice was: "Just what do you do for a living?"

"I am a private investigator; people hire me to handle their private matters."

"How long have you been a private investigator?"

"For a little over twenty five years."

"How did you meet the deceased?"

"He was looking for someone that was really good in my line of work, and he hired me."

"How long did you work for the deceased?"

"Ten years and counting."

"Why did the deceased feel the need to hire a P.I., and what purpose did he hire you for?"

"His daughter and her husband were said to have died in a mere car accident, and the case was closed. But Mr. Osbourne didn't believe it; he felt that they had been murdered."

"Were you able to prove that they were murdered?"

"Not when I first took this case. We had a lot of leads, but they never panned out or they lead to yet another dead end. But, in the last couple of months I was able find all the proof we needed."

"Objection, Your Honor."

"On what grounds Mr. Prod?"

"Hearsay, there has been no proof of that given as evidence to this court."

"Overruled for now, this court will wait and see what kind of proof there is. Mr. Straitway please continue with this witness."

"When did you tell Mr. Osbourne about your findings?"

"The evening before he died."

"Did the deceased tell what he was going to do with the information you gave him?"

"Mr. Osbourne said he was about to make a lot of changes. What kind of changes?"

"To his will and other things."

"Do you have proof of this conversation?"

"Yes, I do."

"Your Honor the defense would like to offer these documents into evidence as Exhibits #5, #6, and #7."

"So noted, they will become evidence in these trial proceedings."

"What does all of this have to do with this trial?"

"Well like I said, and the late Mr. Osbourne believed, you wouldn't have one case without the other one. Soon as I told him about my findings, Mr. Osbourne offered me another case."

"You said that the deceased wanted you to hire you for another case?"

"Yes he did."

"What was the case?"

"His murder, and to prove who murdered him."

"Objection, Your Honor."

"On what grounds Mr. Prod?"

"Hearsay, we already have our murderer over there; the defendant, her and all of her crazy beliefs."

"Overruled, and Mr. Prod you will watch yourself. And if there is another outburst from you, you will be found in contempt of this court."

Right then Mr. Straitway called for an objection. The judge asked the defense attorney to continue. "Your Honor, the defense would like to place these envelopes and their contents as evidence in this trial as Exhibits #8 and #9. Is this your signature on these documents?" he asked Mr Brice.

"Yes it is."

"How, why, and when did the deceased hire you for my client, the defendant?"

"Because he left me a letter in one those envelopes to that effect."

The judge said "so noted, they will become evidence in this trial proceeding."

Mr Brice continued. "He had a feeling that she would be accused of his murder."

"What were your instructions?"

"To find any and every one involved with his murder, and help the authorities bring them to justice."

"What type of other information do you have concerning this case?"

"I have information about a Mr. Ned Taylor."

"Who is this person Ned Taylor and what does he have to with this trial?"

"He was hired to get close to the defendant the best way he knew how, and plant false information on her person, in her apartment, and in her truck to implicate her in the murder of Mr. Osbourne."

"Do you have any proof of this?"

"His sworn statement is in that group of notarized documents that you just placed in evidence."

"So why didn't Mr. Osbourne hire someone else for the defendant, and allow you to finish the case you've worked on for so long?"

"The reason he hired me is that the same people that murdered him also murdered his daughter and son in law, and attempted to murder his only grandchild as well."

Mr. Prod jumped up and started yelling objections out from everywhere. The judge overruled him. Then Judge Watts asked Mr. Prod to control himself and wait until the witness was finished answering the question. The judge then turned to the witness and asked Mr. Brice to please continue because the court was very interested in his findings.

Mr. Brice picked up right where he had left off, "… and Mr. Osbourne knew that I could and would complete the task. In our last conversation, when we talked about his upcoming murder, he informed me he had left me a trail of breadcrumbs; well, really the whole loaf. Mr. Osbourne wanted me to solve his murder, and make sure those that had taken part in it 'pay for what they had done and pay dearly,' those were his exact words."

"Mr. Brice can you please shed some light on it for this court?"

"Yes, if you will hand me those papers that you placed into evidence I have my mark on. I will read them for this court.

"The rest is told in this notarized statement I got from the man that pulled Geneva to safety. 'They had ran off the road and hit a very large tree on the right side of the road. I was driving from the other direction when I heard a loud crash. That is how I happened upon the accident, as it had just taken place. As I was approaching it, I called for emergency help and gave them directions to the accident.' He said that he saw flames were coming out from under the hood of the car. He tried to get the driver free but his leg was caught and pinned down by something, with the steering wheel pushed into his chest, and he said that he was in a lot of pain. 'I felt that he knew he wasn't going to make it even if I were able to free him. Yet I continued to try to free him. Once he looked over at his wife, and he realized that she was already gone. I saw the tears running down his face as he asked me to please get their precious daughter, Geneva out of the car to safety. Shouting "please hurry, save our baby. She still has so much to live for." Once I got the child out of the car, and we were a safe distance way, the car exploded into even a bigger blaze and it was burning fast, as the wind was high that day. When the emergency teams arrived they put the flames out, but there was nothing that they could do for the man and his wife, the two of them had perished in the fire. The firemen said that they were burned a little above a crisp. Officer Planker asked me a lot of questions and took down all my contact information.' Since the accident Officer Planker has retired to Florida, and some of the files for Rebecca and Freddrick Trice's accident were missing. The man could only tell them what he had seen, and after he did they thanked him for being a Good Samaritan, and they let him go."

Then Mr. Straitway interjected "and thanks to some great P.I. work by Mr. Brice, the mysterious stranger has a name, and it is Mr. Quincy Booth. You can continue Mr. Brice, and he then read another one of the letters."

He said that the late Mr. Osbourne wrote in this letter:

Dear Mr. Brice,

In the case of my untimely death, please look very closely at my son Theodore in particular, and all of his personal affairs. Check all his accounts, follow the trail of money, my blood will lead you to him. I have always known that he had something to do with my darling Rebecca's death!

I know that he could and would, if he were given the chance and under the right circumstances, he will eventually kill me or have me killed. He will lead you to everyone that is involved. I suspect my attorney; Mr. Johns is involved as well. I have been changing my will a lot lately, and I noticed that he has had me signing two different wills each time I sign them. I tested my theory a month or so ago, I asked him to get a book for me across from me in my library. While his back was turned, I peeked at the papers underneath. I have never let on to him that I saw the other wills, nor that I suspect him of any wrongdoing. But the changes that I have been making, they would cause the killer or killers to play his or her hand soon. I know that Odessa would be blamed because of her friendship with me. I know that she has been resented from the first day of her employment. She is hated because she reminds Teddy of the relationship that I had with his sister, my daughter Rebecca. Watch out for Teddy, he has a very mean streak. I don't know how far he will go; I pray for him every day. I hope that there is something good left deep down on the inside of him. Maybe his love for Geneva will be enough for him to stop all of this. I already know how much he hates me. Odessa has my will in her possession, but she doesn't even know it. I gave it to her to put it away somewhere safe, where no one else would find it. It is my only real Last Will and Testament. I had another law firm to draw it up for me. Odessa is one of my true friends, she and Oscar. Oscar has some of the other pieces to this puzzle; he will give them to you upon your request. I have given him instructions to follow, and I know that I can trust him to do as I have asked. I trust Oscar with my very life. I know that I'm playing a dangerous game and that I am pushing someone over the edge. If there is one thing that I have learned in this life and that I am certain of, is they will play and they will show their hand. If Odessa has been arrested for my murder please show this letter to the presiding judge, he will know what to do. Also, take all the papers I gave Odessa and any new evidence with you. Please tell Odessa to remember my last words; they will help you if you have any doubts. Tell her to tell you all about the last day and hours of my life.

Sincerely,
Mr. Harrington Osbourne, III.

Then Mr. Brice read a short portion of Mr. O's Last Will and Testament. After he finished, Mr. Straitway said he didn't have any more questions for this witness. Judge Watts said, "cross Mr. Prod?"

"Yes, Your Honor. Mr. Brice, please be honest with yourself and tell this court where you really got your information from, and who really hired and paid you! The defendant-- (pointing at Odessa) she did, didn't she? And she paid you to tell all those lies to this court!"

"Objection, Your Honor, Mr. Prod is badgering the witness."

Then Mr. Prod said he'd withdraw his question, "I have no more questions for this witness." The judge asked Mr. Brice to step down, then he asked Mr. Straitway to call the defense's next witness. He said "the defense has no more witnesses. We rest, your Honor."

Once the defense team rested, Mr. Prod became visibly upset because the defense didn't put Odessa on the stand. He wanted a chance to get at her; he wanted to attack her, her beliefs, her church, and her family.

Judge Watts said he wanted both sides to be ready to present their closing remarks tomorrow. Then he said "the court is dismissed until ten a.m. tomorrow." The bailiff asked everyone to rise as Judge Watts left the courtroom.

"This is anchor Darwine Trestor and co-anchor Ms. Veronica Best, reporting to you live from WNT Worldly News Tonight, bringing you the updates from the trial today. Mr. Straitway had yet another surprise witness for the prosecution. A private investigator named Mr. Brice, and boy was he good; no he wasn't good, he was great on the stand. He'd been working for the deceased for ten years, and from what we were lead to believe today, is that he is still working for him. Wow, check that out; the deceased still has people on his payroll. He said that the defendant was innocent; well, Mr. Brice didn't, but apparently the deceased said so. He had a lot of proof to back up what he was saying from the stand. He even read a notarized letter from the deceased, informing everyone of who would murder him. The defense team did a great job, didn't they? (Applauding) Now, to all of our viewers out there, you all heard us say on this station the prosecution better watch out. We tried to tell them that Mr. Straitway just may turn out be a worthy opponent, and he has proven that he is. (More applauding) I bet the prosecution didn't even see what was coming at them these last two days. (Laughter) I know they are really working hard tonight and going through everything with a fine tooth comb. Prosecutor Prod, if you know like we do, you better bring everything that you have in that little black bag of tricks with you. I have a feeling that you may need them for your closing remarks. (Laughing in the station) Kudos to you attorney Straitway! Now go for the jugular if you know how. This is anchor Darwine Trestor and co-anchor Veronica Best saying, Goodnight to all of our great viewers and great listeners. We here at WNT, Worldly News Tonight love you all. Again goodnight."

Mr. Straitway and his team are getting together everything that has gone on in the trial. He is preparing the defense's closing remarks.

Mr. Prod is still mad, and he is taking out a lot of his frustrations on his team. Someone from his team got so upset with him and his pushy ways, they decided to leak to the press some of his underhanded and unethical practices.

Court is in session and it is time for closing remarks. Judge Watts asked if the prosecution was ready to give its closing remarks. Mr. Prod said "yes we are, your Honor" and stepped right up to the jury box, looking each one up and down. Then Mr. Prod said "the prosecution feels that we have proven our case beyond reasonable doubt. We showed you that the deceased, Mr. Harrington Osbourne, III, was murdered by the defendant. She had the motive: you heard from some of our witnesses that the deceased cut her out of his will. The deceased, a kind and loving employer, died at the hands of his so called 'trusted nurse and friend.' (Pointing at Odessa) You heard from one of the county's trusted community members, coroner Dr. Scott Trixion, say the poison that was found in the deceased's body was the very same poison that was on all the patches. You do remember what Detective Rodgers said-- that she had sticky residue on her hands. That caused them to get several search warrants, to search her room in the mansion, her apartment in the city, and her truck. In their search for the truth, they found more patches in both residences with the poison on them. Then they found a valve of that same poison in the trunk of her truck, under the flap inside her spare tire. They also found several wills that she had been making changes to. Then they found a threatening letter to the deceased. The defense team will say that she is innocent. Are we to take the word of the butler? They are friends, he probably helped her plan it. Maybe he was cut out the will, too. They said the deceased prayed for his son everyday; he probably was praying for his son's help with the two of them. They will say our evidence is all fabricated. They will say they don't know who changed those wills, or who wrote the letters. I tell you that the defendant, Ms. Odessa Princeton, took advantage of the deceased. All her talk of the Bible and the mere thought of her being a Christian. That's why the deceased didn't take his meds; she was killing him already! He was helpless and already dying and she knew that, but she couldn't wait just a few lousy months for him to die on his own. Please pay attention to all the evidence the defense has. It's all hearsay, and everything they have told you or shown you in this trial is a bunch of circumstantial evidence. I tell you, the defense is trying to brainwash you. The defense thinks that you all are stupid, deaf, dumb, and blind. But we, the prosecution, we know that you are all very intelligent and that you are all able to think for yourselves. We also feel that once you all look at the evidence again, you must bring back a guilty verdict, convict her of this premeditated murder, and give her the death penalty. I rest my case, your Honor."

Judge Watts called for the defense attorney to give his closing remarks. Mr. Straitway started out by saying "we the defense wouldn't dare add insult to injury (as he looked at the 12 jurors). Mr. Prod and the rest of the prosecution team have tried to play tricks with your minds. We, the defense believe that you all are very intelligent people, and that you understand that this case before you today is not whether the deceased was murdered, but who murdered him. The prosecution has insinuated that you, the jury, weren't capable of thinking for yourselves. But the defense feels that you are all educated and upstanding citizens of this state. The defendant went to school to become a nurse to save lives, not to take them. You have heard from the prosecution, saying the butler was in on it; but the fact is that the deceased called him a trusted friend, in whom he trusted his very life and to carry out his last wishes. You have heard Mr. Harrington Osbourne, III speak from the grave, telling you who murdered him but also who didn't. The deceased said he and the defendant were friends, and she was hated for it and not for her beliefs. The deceased said he feared for his life, but not from the defendant, from his son, his own flesh and blood. Our only job here is to show you all that there is reasonable doubt, and to show that the prosecution's case has a lot of holes in it. We are confident you will bring back a verdict of 'not guilty' and set this loving, caring, young woman free, and allow this state to pursue the real murderer or murderers of Mr. Harrington Osbourne, III."

The judge admonished the jury that they must either find the defendant innocent or guilty, using only the truth that was presented in the case. "The evidence is the only thing that you are allowed to use to come up with the verdict of innocent or guilty."

During the jury's deliberations, Juror #3's job was to always cause a lot of confusion and chaos in the jury room. She was one of Mr. Prod's favorites. Trust me; she was so good at her job she was receiving a check as often as the people that were really on the payroll. Juror #5, this was only his third time working for the prosecution, but he did have a big part to play. He and juror #3 were supposed to follow the lead of juror #8. These were some of Mr. Prod's specially hand-picked jurors, paid for this and other trials. Now Juror #8 was really the one in charge, or so he thought. They would find out later that the foreman was really and truly in charge. Juror #3's job was to plant negative thoughts in the heads of each juror about the defendant so they would vote against her. This was his job every time he was on a jury. He did his job so well he was paid five thousand dollars up front, and five thousand more when the job was done. He came from another big city where he did the same thing. One of Mr. Prod's associates turned him on to juror #8, almost at onset of his career. Mr. Prod has been under Federal investigation for some time now.

His team of jurors were up to no good in the jury room, and they kept up their stuff for one day and twenty two hours, to be exact. They acted as if they were on some kind of drugs. Each time the foreman would call for a vote, they would go into action. But when the foreman called for the vote this time, they didn't know they had been fired from their jobs as Mr. Prod's jurors. The foreman asked everyone to settle down and look at the evidence clearly. She pointed at each piece of evidence, one at a time, and discussed it. Then when it was time to vote, they got ready to start up again. But juror #9 o all over the j had a verdict. each a verdict.

After days and nights of deliberating, the jury reached a verdict. Everyone was notified and returned to the courtroom. Judge Watts asked the bailiff to let all the jurors into the courtroom. As they came in and began to take their seats, Mr. Prod looked as if he has seen a ghost. He became white as a sheet; it seemed that all of his blood just drained from his face. He tried to read jurors #3, #5, and #8's faces, but they kept avoiding eye contact with him. He knew then that wasn't a good sign.

Once all the jurors were seated the judge asked the foreman if they were able to reach a verdict. She answered yes. The judge then asked for the verdict, and she handed it to the bailiff, and he handed it to the judge. Judge Watts read the verdict and passed it back to the foreman and asked her to read it. The Judge asked that the defendant please stand during the reading of the verdict. When the verdict was read, the courtroom went up in an uproar. Judge Watts asked everyone to please take their seats and to please quiet down, as he thanked the jury for a job well done. But Mr. Prod wasn't satisfied; he wanted to poll the jury. Judge Watts allowed it, and Mr. Prod found out his people had really voted against him; no one does that to the great Mr. Prod and gets away with it. Judge Watts dismissed everyone and said "this case is over. The defendant is free to leave." Mr. Prod was very angry, he didn't stand for betrayal.

Outside the courthouse, the reporters are all crowding around, trying to get a statement so they can meet their respective deadlines. Mr. Straitway began to speak as he grabbed hold of Odessa's hand. He told the reporters and everyone standing outside listening, that Odessa has been declaring her innocence from day one. "She has also remained steadfast in her beliefs, which the prosecution tried to use against her. But the One that she tells everyone that she meets about has not only freed her, but he has vindicated her and caused her to triumph over all those that were persecuting her." Mr. Straitway raised both their hands in the air and shouted "we have prevailed with God's help. We have prevailed!"

When the jurors were dismissed, the feds arrested jurors #3, #5, and #8. The Feds have also arrested and have taken Mr. Prod into custody. After Prod's arrest, the court house grapevine got the news; the word on the circuit was the prosecution office were going start reopening all of his old cases and looking at the recent ones as well-- not just some of them, but all of them. They say that he has been stacking up books against other people and getting paid to do so.

The bus loaded with prisoners left the Cook County jail at 6 a.m. it was traveling on I-90 on the way to the Pontiac Prison in Pontiac, Illinois, when they received a call over the radio informing them that one of the prisoners was not on the bus. The guard asked the dispatcher how that could be, seeing that they took a head-count before they drove out of the gate. The dispatcher said that they needed to pull off the road onto the shoulder and do another head count, and check each prisoners I.D bands. Sure enough, the count was right but there was one wrong prisoner.

They put out an A.P.B. stating there was an escapee on the loose, and he has vowed to make everyone pay that had a hand in sending him to jail, or anyone that was remotely connected to it.

The End

CPSIA information can be obtained
at www.ICGtesting.com
Printed in the USA
BVHW04s0824260718
522709BV00003B/6/P

9 781640 880610